"No, call me and I'll come get you."

He kissed Jules on the cheek, and she leaned into him and rested her head on his chest as if it was a respite from all of her worries. His arms went around her and pulled her close. She felt good there, and he realized he was relieved that she wasn't engaged to someone else. It wasn't fair for him to want her all to himself, but in the heat of the moment, he hadn't been feeling rational. He pushed the perplexing thought aside and simply held her, losing himself in her nearness.

Then a voice sounded over the hospital's intercom system, startling him back to the present.

"I'll be waiting for your call," he said as he put some distance between them.

She made a face that suggested she might object, but then she said, "Thanks, Owen. What would I do without you?"

As they each turned and walked in separate directions—she toward the elevator and him toward the entrance—he found himself thinking he'd never want to put that theory to the test.

Dear Reader,

What's better than a friends-to-lovers story? How about best friends who fall in love after pretending to be engaged? Because who would make a better fake fiancé than your best friend? He or she knows you so well.

Juliette Kingsbury and Owen McFadden have known each other most of their lives. Juliette's mother's fondest wish is to see her daughter married. When she falls ill, Juliette will do anything to lift her mom's spirits. Then Owen, who needs a way to prove that he and his company are good investment risks, suggests an engagement of convenience, and the two shock everyone by taking their friendship to the next level. Who knew all it would take was a fake commitment to make them realize their soulmates had been right beside them all along.

I hope you enjoy Juliette and Owen's story, the final book in the McFaddens of Tinsley Cove trilogy—and my 40th novel for Harlequin—as much as I loved writing it.

Please keep in touch. I love to hear from readers.

Warmly,

Nancy

Instagram: @NancyRThompson

Facebook: /NRobardsThompson

Website: NancyRobardsThompson.com

RULES OF ENGAGEMENT

NANCY ROBARDS THOMPSON

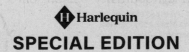

SPECIAL EDITION

Harlequin®
SPECIAL EDITION™

Recycling programs for this product may not exist in your area.

ISBN-13: 978-1-335-59473-0

Rules of Engagement

For questions and comments about the quality of this book, please contact us at CustomerService@Harlequin.com.

TM and ® are trademarks of Harlequin Enterprises ULC.

 Harlequin Enterprises ULC
22 Adelaide St. West, 41st Floor
Toronto, Ontario M5H 4E3, Canada
www.Harlequin.com

Printed in Lithuania

MIX
Paper | Supporting responsible forestry
FSC® C021394

USA TODAY bestselling author **Nancy Robards Thompson** has a degree in journalism. She worked as a newspaper reporter until she realized reporting "just the facts" was boring. Happier to report to her muse, Nancy has found Nirvana writing women's fiction, romance and cozy mysteries full-time. Critics have deemed her work "funny, smart and observant." She lives in Tennessee with her husband and their corgi. For more, please visit her website at nancyrobardsthompson.com.

Books by Nancy Robards Thompson

Harlequin Special Edition

The McFaddens of Tinsley Cove

Selling Sandcastle
Rules of Engagement

The Savannah Sisters

A Down-Home Savannah Christmas
Southern Charm & Second Chances
Her Savannah Surprise

Celebration, TX

The Cowboy's Runaway Bride
A Bride, a Barn, and a Baby
The Cowboy Who Got Away

The Fortunes of Texas: The Secret Fortunes

Fortune's Surprise Engagement

The Fortunes of Texas: Rambling Rose

Betting on a Fortune

The Fortunes of Texas: Digging for Secrets

Worth a Fortune

Visit the Author Profile page
at Harlequin.com for more titles.

Rules of Engagement marks my 40th novel for Harlequin. It's dedicated to Gail Chasan, who bought my first book, and all the lovely readers who read my books. Much love to all!

Chapter One

"Oh, just try it on for fun, honey," said longtime Tinsley Cove resident Helen Kingsbury. "Humor me. Is it such a crime that I want to see my daughter in a wedding dress while I can still remember what she looks like in it?"

"Are you really playing that card, Mom?" Juliette Kingsbury forced a smile and did her best to infuse enough good humor into her words to not make her mother feel bad, but the truth was, Juliette was still reeling from the bombshell her mother had dropped at lunch not even an hour ago.

Earlier that morning, Juliette had flown in on the red-eye from Los Angeles. She was exhausted and had wanted nothing more than a hot shower and a couple of hours of sleep, but no sooner had she stashed her bags in her room at her mother's house, than her mother had insisted they go to lunch. She really wasn't hungry, but she had relented. Plus, since they'd had lunch out, she had decided to pick up the check. After all, she was the one with the well-paying Hollywood job.

Or at least she used to be. Until everything fell apart.

But her mom had wanted lunch, and Juliette had

needed to go downtown to try on her bridesmaid dress for her best friend Natasha Allen's wedding anyway. *Why not?* she'd thought. *It would be nice to treat Mom to lunch.*

Juliette hadn't wanted to dip into her rainy day fund. She'd still had a little room on her credit card…even after charging the bridesmaid dress, buying the plane ticket home and taking a rideshare in from the airport. Living in LA wasn't cheap, but at least she had an affordable living situation. For the past seven years, she'd been sharing a three-bedroom bungalow in North Hollywood with an older woman named Ingrid and her much-younger boyfriend, Harry. The three of them had become close friends.

Since she had ordered a side salad, she'd told her mom to order anything she wanted on the menu. Later, she'd buy groceries for the rest of the week and insist that she was starving for her mom's home cooking, which was true.

Oh, and she still had to pick up a wedding gift for Natasha and Jack. She still couldn't believe they were getting married. Their relationship had been on and off since high school. They'd finally realized they couldn't live without each other

"And don't even get me started on Forest McFadden eloping," her mother had said at lunch as Juliette buttered her second piece of bread. She'd figured if she ate enough bread and drank enough water, the salad would be plenty… At least her bridesmaid dress would fit.

"Of all three McFadden brothers, I thought he'd be the one who had the big traditional wedding," Juliette had said. When she'd looked up, she'd seen the faraway look in her mother's eyes. When she'd asked her if she was okay, her mom had put her hand on Juliette's and said, "Honey, I have some bad news. It's my heart."

And right there in the middle of Le Marais restaurant, her mother had told her about the diagnosis— bradycardia.

As Juliette had digested the words, the world had blurred around her.

"Are you going to get a second opinion?" Juliette had asked.

Her mother had simply shrugged and forked a large bite of croque monsieur into her mouth.

Juliette had set down the bread on her plate, suddenly unable to stomach another bite.

"Mom, I really hope you'll get another opinion. Sometimes doctors make mistakes."

She had promised to consider it, but in the meantime, she would take the prescribed medication, and had insisted she felt fine. It was just that she got tired easily and sometimes forgot things.

Now, as they stood in Primrose Bridal Shop, a few doors down from where they'd eaten lunch, Juliette would've done anything her sweet mother had asked.

It had seemed harmless when her mother urged her to try on a wedding dress *just for fun*. Sort of like playing dress-up.

The thing Juliette hadn't counted on was how emotional her mother would get when Juliette stepped out of the fitting room and onto the dais in front of the trifold mirror in that ridiculously big confection of a gown.

"Oooh!" Helen covered her mouth with her hands. "You look...beautiful. Like a real, live princess. Just look at you."

Then her mom started crying. No, cry wasn't the right word for it. Helen blubbered full-body sobs, her mascara and her nose running in unison.

"Mom. Mom, it's okay," Juliette said, grabbing a wad of tissues from the box on the table next to one of the chairs and gently dabbing at her mother's face. She did her best to avoid getting mascara streaks on the ivory silk shantung and lace when her mother pulled her into a hug. Juliette patted her on the back and said, "Please don't cry. I never would've put on the dress if I'd known it would upset you so much."

"I'm not upset." A shuddering breath followed her declaration. "Really, I'm not. I just never thought I'd live to see this day." Helen pulled away and held Juliette at arm's length. "I just have to look at you. You'll look beautiful when you walk down the aisle."

"Mom? You realize I'm just trying on the dress. I'm not really getting married. I'm here for Natasha's wedding."

Helen blanched. "Of course. I want to commit this moment to memory because by the time you finally do get married, I probably won't be able to remember it. If I'm here at all. I'm sorry to cause such a scene."

With that, Helen dissolved into another ugly cry, pulling her daughter close again.

It was heartbreaking, seeing her sweet mother this way. Truth be told, Juliette would've said anything to comfort her.

"Mom, you'll be here for my wedding."

Helen jerked back and looked at Juliette.

"What do you mean?" her mom asked, looking hopeful for the first time since Juliette had gotten home.

Yeah, what do I mean?

"Is there something you're not telling me?" Helen persisted. There was a sparkle in her eyes that made Juliette at once happy and heartbroken. Happy to see her so hopeful. Heartbroken at the thought of quashing her mom's delight.

But maybe she didn't have to.

"Well, my wedding might not be as far off as you think."

Helen gasped. "Have you met someone? You've met someone, haven't you?"

Before Juliette could answer, Claudia, the shop owner who had helped Juliette with the bridesmaid dress and the wedding gown try-on, came over to check on them.

Helen grabbed the woman's hands and cried, "My daughter has met someone!"

When Claudia shot Juliette a questioning look, all Juliette could do was smile and cross her fingers behind her back as she said, "I've met someone."

Inwardly, Juliette cringed at the thought of her mother seeing the gesture in the mirror behind her and because she was just about as single as an unattached woman could be, given that she hadn't had a real date in a long time and had no viable prospects even on the distant horizon. It was difficult to maintain romantic relationships when you worked in film and television. Los Angeles was her home base, but she had to travel where the work took her.

"Why is this the first I'm hearing of this beau of yours?" Helen asked, holding on to both of Juliette's hands.

"Well, I didn't want to say anything until I was certain that it would work out."

Ugh. Rein it in, Juliette. Don't write dream checks that your reality can't cash.

"So, it's serious?" Helen asked, so giddy she was almost breathless.

"Let me get out of this dress and we can talk about it. Okay?"

Helen nodded, wringing her hands the whole while.

Good, Juliette thought. As she stepped off the platform, she racked her brain for an exit strategy. She had to come up with something before she dug herself in deeper.

At least she hadn't said she was engaged. Thank goodness. That would be a bridge too far, and it would be too messy, too heartbreaking for her mother when the inevitable *breakup* happened down the road.

Her mom beamed at her from the chair across from the mirrors. She looked so darned happy.

As Juliette smiled back, she silently reasoned there was no harm in letting her mom believe that she'd met someone special. Was there? Just this week, while she was at home.

Plus, an added bonus would be that her mother wouldn't try to set her up with a date for this weekend's wedding. Her other best friend, Owen McFadden, was one of the groomsmen and just as single as she was. She planned to hang out with him during her visit.

As she turned to go into the dressing room so she could get out of the gown, the bell on the door jingled. A tall, thin woman with a sleek platinum bob stepped inside the shop.

"I have an eleven o'clock appointment for a fitting. I'm late. I know," she said to Claudia. "I just got into town."

That voice.

Juliette turned around to look, but the woman's back was to her. That voice sounded so familiar. Dread settled over Juliette like a weighted blanket.

It can't be.

Please don't let it be.

As if sensing that she was being watched, the woman turned around and impaled Juliette with an icy blue glare.

Juliette's stomach spiraled.

Kimmy Ogilvie.

Of course. She's a bridesmaid in the wedding, too.

Since Kimmy had come in from out of town, she had to pick up her dress just as Juliette had needed to get hers. But why did Kimmy have to show up at the precise moment that Juliette looked like an idiot wearing this giant meringue of a dress?

Of all the people in Tinsley Cove.

In high school, she and Kimmy had traveled in separate but overlapping circles. Juliette had grown up next door to Natasha, the bride. She was the common link in the Venn diagram of high school friendships. Well, Natasha and Owen McFadden were the links, but Owen was a story for another day.

If Juliette had known she'd run into her former nemesis, she would've never agreed to try on the bridal gown.

It was humiliating. Thirty-one-year-old women didn't try on wedding gowns for fun. Looking at it through the eyes of Kimmy, a person who used to get a charge out of seeing Juliette fail, it felt…kind of pathetic.

Or it would be, if Kimmy knew that Juliette had just lied to her mother about being almost engaged… but Kimmy didn't know. And if Juliette hurried into the fitting room and changed into her own clothes, she could tell Kimmy she was here to pick up her bridesmaid dress, then she could get the heck out of Primrose Bridal Shop and pretend like this never happened.

But no such luck.

"Juliette Kingsbury, is that you?" Kimmy gushed, turning on a sickeningly sweet charm that totally belied the evil glare Juliette had seen in Kimmy's first reaction.

Alas, there was no escape, Juliette realized. She smiled to keep herself from grinding her molars.

"It's me, live and in person," Juliette said, mustering all the confidence she didn't feel, but wished she had. Why did she let this woman make her feel fifteen again? "I didn't recognize you at first, Kimmy. You've changed your hair."

When they were in high school, Kimmy used to be a dark-blonde surfer chick wannabe, with rope curls that flowed down her back and a boho style that was more thrift store than the fashion plate who was standing right in front of her.

Back in the day, Kimmy hadn't surfed, she'd lounged around in her tiny bikini and baked in the sun until her olive skin was the perfect shade of bronze—all the while keeping a close eye on Owen McFadden.

They'd been a thing for an excruciating two years, but at the end of their sophomore year, Owen had come to his senses and had broken up with her, confiding in Juliette that Kimmy had been too clingy. He had just needed some breathing room.

For Juliette, being relegated to the friend zone by Owen had been both a curse and a blessing. On one hand, they hung out and he confided in her—even while he and Kimmy were dating, which was one of the reasons Kimmy had always hated her. But on the other hand, the painful truth was that Juliette had been in love with Owen since elementary school, and he'd never seen her as girlfriend material.

To Owen, she'd always been one of the guys...except for that one night when she'd driven him home after the graduation kegger on the beach—he'd had too much beer to drive. She hadn't tasted a drop. After she'd helped him out of the car and up to his front door, he'd kissed her and declared that if they were both still single when they were really old...like thirty...that they should get married because she understood him. She was his best friend.

He'd never mentioned it again. Not even over the years that they'd kept in touch.

Juliette hadn't thought about that night in a long time. It had been the beer talking, putting words in Owen's mouth. Emotions had been running high because she was going away to college and he was going to school close to home. What was the sense in dwelling on something that would never happen?

"*Hello?* Juliette? Where did you go?"

Kimmy had moved from the sales desk to the fitting room area and was standing with her hands on her slim hips, looking annoyed. Helen had gotten up from her seat to join them, too.

"Sorry, I was, uh… What were you saying?"

"I was saying, people call me Kimberly now."

She smoothed a hand over her shiny platinum locks as she gave Juliette an appraising once-over. "Time marches on. We've all grown up and changed. Well, except for you. You look exactly the same, Juliette."

It was a backhanded compliment if there had been one.

Kimmy's perfectly shaped right brow arched and she wagged a French-manicured index finger at the dress. "Are congratulations in order?"

"They certainly are," Helen said. "Juliette just surprised me with the fabulous news that she's engaged to a wonderful man. She's getting married."

Oh, no, Mom…that's not what I said.

Both Juliette and Kimmy looked at Helen, who stood there beaming, her eyes bright with unshed happy tears.

Juliette was just opening her mouth to set the record straight, when Helen added, "I can't remember when I've ever been this happy. My baby girl is finally going to be a bride. She is so career focused—you know she works in the movies, right? Well, she does, but I never thought I'd live to see this day. This is proof that miracles really do happen."

"Congratulations," Kimmy said. "Will I meet your fiancé at the wedding?"

Luckily, Kimmy didn't give Juliette time to answer. "I know firsthand what an exciting time it is when you get engaged."

Kimmy lifted a hand and flashed a diamond so big it could've been a bauble on a chandelier. "I'm engaged, too. We may have had our differences when we were younger, but we always did seem to be on the same trajectory. Didn't we?"

If you're talking about Owen McFadden... "Yes, we did."

Sort of.

Kimmy's expectant gaze dropped to Juliette's left hand, which Juliette promptly tucked into the folds of the gown's voluminous skirt, as she racked her brain for a way out of this predicament.

The sensible thing to do would be to set the record straight. She wasn't engaged... In fact, she was as single as single could be, even if she was wearing a bridal gown.

Her mother was holding Kimmy's hand, gushing over the rock on her ring finger. A bauble that brilliant could've fed a starving nation.

Envy gnawed at Juliette's insides.

Everything Kimmy Ogilvie had ever done had always been bigger and better than Juliette's best efforts...really everyone's efforts, for that matter. Kimmy had gotten into Juliette's first-choice college. Juliette had been the understudy to Kimmy's Maria in the senior class production of *The Sound of Music*. After Juliette had announced to their group of mutual friends that she was going to run for junior class president, Kimmy decided to run for the same office. Kimmy won because, the day of the election, she gave away free sodas retrofitted with a label that said Vote for Kimmy and Life Will Always Be Sweet and Bubbly!

All that aside, the only thing that mattered was that Kimmy had captured Owen's heart. Juliette would've traded all that other stuff if Owen would've had feelings for her.

"I suppose I'll see you at the drinks party tonight at the Allens' place," Kimmy said. "I haven't told Tasha the good news yet." Kimmy stared dreamily at the sparkler on her left hand. "I can't wait to see the look on her face. Have you told her your news yet?"

Juliette shook her head. "I don't want to steal her thunder. This weekend is about her. Maybe we should save our news for after the wedding?"

Kimmy raised a brow as if the thought had never occurred to her. "I suppose you're right." She laughed. "Well, then, I guess you and I have a secret, don't we?"

A few minutes later, Juliette was finally free of the cursed wedding dress. As she stepped out of the shop onto Main Street, she squinted into the afternoon sun and mentally tried on different ways to gently suggest to her mother that she keep the news of the, um…engagement under wraps for a while. Better yet, she should just come clean and tell her mother she'd misunderstood. She wasn't engaged…or even dating anyone. But she couldn't come up with the right words.

She'd talk to her mom after they got home. In the

meantime, Juliette had steeled herself for her mother to pump her for the details—a name, a photo, background info. But Helen was strangely silent. In fact, she wasn't walking beside Juliette anymore; she'd fallen a few paces behind.

"Sorry, am I walking too fast?" When Juliette turned to her mother, she noticed that Helen's complexion looked a frightening shade of gray.

"Mom? Are you okay?"

Helen swayed, and Juliette took her arm. "Mom?"

"I don't feel well. Maybe I should sit down?"

Helen leaned into Juliette, who walked her mother to a bench between the bridal shop and the restaurant.

"Mom? What's wrong? How do you feel bad?"

Helen didn't answer her. She slumped down onto the bench and seemed to sway in and out of consciousness.

Juliette sat down next to her, holding her up. Her mother's body was limp and clammy.

"I'm okay," Helen said. "I'm just a little lightheaded."

"I'm calling 911, Mom."

"No, do not call 911," Helen insisted. "I just need to sit here for a minute."

"Mom, I think you should go to the hospital." Juliette's voice shook and beads of perspiration broke out on her forehead as she fished in her purse for her phone. "What if you're having a stroke?"

"I'll go to the hospital, but not in an ambulance. Do you understand me?"

"I can't leave you sitting here while I get the car, Mom."

Juliette looked around to see if she recognized anyone who could sit with her mother while she ran the two or three blocks for the car.

"Jules, is that you?" A familiar voice broke through her mind's haze.

As if she'd conjured him, Juliette saw Owen McFadden sitting in the car that had just stopped on the street in front of them.

"Oh my gosh, Owen," she said. "I'm so happy to see you. Mom isn't feeling well. Will you drive us to the hospital?"

As Owen sat next to Jules on an uncomfortable beige vinyl loveseat in the waiting area of the emergency room, he reached out and rubbed her back. Her elbows were braced on her knees, and she rested her head in her hands. The faint antiseptic smell of cleaning solution mingled with occasional whiffs of alcohol and other disinfectants.

"Hey, she's going to be okay."

Of course, he didn't know that for sure, but Helen had been conscious when they'd arrived. The nurse—he couldn't remember her name, but he was certain she'd gone to the same high school as Jules and him—wouldn't let Jules go back to the treatment area with her. She'd explained that Helen was stable, but they were unusually busy with an overload of patients. There was no room for family members in the exam cubicles. She'd promised to keep them updated as often as she could.

In the meantime, he would wait with Jules until they received word that Helen was in the clear.

It was the least he could do.

A testament to the nurse's claim, the waiting room was crowded with anxious-looking people. Some paced the floor, others fidgeted on the beige vinyl chairs, talking to each other in worried tones or staring off into space. A couple of kids were playing cards while a young woman tried to comfort a crying baby.

Owen turned to Jules and said, "Well, it's good to see you. I wish it wasn't under these circumstances."

Of course, she'd come home to Tinsley Cove for the wedding and he would've seen her there, but he could think of hundreds of happier initial reunion scenarios. As if to second this thought, the overhead fluorescent lights buzzed and cast a harsh glow, creating an uncomfortable, sterile ambience.

"Yeah, hello to you, too," Jules said. "Who knew we'd end up in the emergency room? I think this is a first for us, isn't it? Hard to believe, after all the crazy stuff we did when we were young."

"I guess we were charmed."

"Apparently so." She shook her head. "I can't believe you happened along when you did. I had no idea what I was going to do. Mom didn't want me to call 911, and I didn't want to leave her alone on that bench while I got the car."

"You know me," he said. "I'm always happy to be at your service."

Jules smiled, but it didn't reach her eyes. She was still as beautiful as she'd always been—long curly blond hair, blue-blue eyes, not much makeup. She looked exactly the same as the last time he'd seen her, six months ago, when she'd come to town between film projects to visit her mother. Basically, she looked the same as she had in high school, only more worldly. Even so, the morning's events had clearly taken a toll on her. She looked wrung out.

"When did you get into town?" he asked.

"This morning. I took the red-eye from LAX. It seems like it's been days since I've slept, but I'm glad I got here when I did. Owen, what if this had happened when she was alone?"

"But it didn't." He took her hand, and she closed her fingers over his. "You were there for her and that's what counts."

"I just hope she's okay."

He nodded. "Me, too. I didn't know she'd been sick," Owen said.

"When we were at lunch, she mentioned that the doctor had diagnosed her with bradycardia, which has to do with her heart. I had no idea until today. Also, she said she's been having trouble remembering things." Jules shrugged. "I would've come home sooner if I'd known something was wrong."

"Don't beat yourself up. You're here now."

They sat in silence for a moment.

"I appreciate all you've done, but you don't have to wait here with me," she said. "This will probably take a while. I can get a cab or an Uber back to my car. I'm sure you have a million things to do."

Owen shook his head. "I picked up my suit for the wedding yesterday. I don't have to be anywhere. In fact, there's no place I'd rather be than right here with you."

She slanted a narrow-eyed glance at him as she'd

done so many times in the past. "I don't know whether to be grateful or feel sorry for you since you have nothing else better to do than to sit here with me."

He snorted, happy to see the sense of humor that he loved so much finally surface.

"Gratitude is always a good way to go," he said. "You can make it up to me later."

She laughed and said, "Well, thank you. I'm just saying, this really could take hours."

"Yep. I know, and that's fine."

She rested her head on his shoulder, leaned into him and sighed as if she were letting go of the weight of the world. Then, just as fast, she sat up and said, "I'm just going to go back there and check on her." She pointed to the wooden double doors that separated the patients from their anxious loved ones. Doors that locked automatically and were designed to prohibit people just like Jules from entering the emergency room after they'd been told not to.

"The doors are locked, Jules. You can't get back there."

"I'll scoot in when someone opens the door," she said.

Owen held on to her hand. "And if you do that, they might kick you out of the hospital altogether. Then what would you do?"

She eyed the doors for a moment, then collapsed onto the seat beside him as if thinking better of it.

"Well, sneaking in somewhere I've been told not to go wouldn't be the worst thing I've done today."

"What are you talking about?" Owen asked. "You've

been back in town less than twelve hours and you're already causing trouble?"

Actually, that wasn't Jules's MO at all. Growing up, she'd always been the voice of reason, keeping *him* out of trouble…when she could. One of the reasons he'd always thought she was too good for him.

He shifted in his seat, unsure where that thought had come from.

He cleared his throat. "What did you do?"

"Well, before I get into that, I should tell you I'm engaged."

Owen flinched and something inside of him died.

She smiled up at him, looking smug and proud.

"You're—you're what?" he asked trying to keep his expression neutral.

"I'm engaged."

"To be married?"

She nodded.

"Are you serious? The last time we talked—what? Two weeks ago?—you said you weren't dating anyone. In fact, you said you'd just broken up with Ed."

Owen realized too late that he'd spat out her ex's name like a bite of rotten tuna. He hadn't meant to sound so judgmental.

"Are you jealous?" she asked. "Because you totally sound jealous."

"No. I am not jealous. I'm…happy for you."

"Liar."

There was a mischievous glint in her eyes. Was she playing him?

Just two weeks ago, he'd asked her if Ed would be her

plus-one for the wedding. She'd said they'd broken up. When he'd tried to comfort her, she'd assured him she was fine. She said she and Ed had never been that serious. It was more of a relationship of convenience. They'd gotten involved after spending the better part of a year together working on a couple of films. They'd been attracted to each other, and one had thing led to another.

But after their last project had wrapped, Ed had hired on with a picture that was filming in Morocco. There hadn't been a place in the crew for Juliette, so she'd stayed behind in LA. Their relationship had cooled faster than a forgotten cup of coffee. Then he'd hired her to work on another film, but that had fallen through. He couldn't remember the details.

"Did you guys get back together?"

She raised her brows. "Who says I'm engaged to Ed?"

"If it's not Ed, that means you're marrying someone you've been serious about for less than a fortnight."

She snorted. "A fortnight? Who are you? Mr. Darcy?"

Fortnight was not a word he usually tossed around. He'd said it because he knew it would make her laugh, and he'd hoped it would draw attention away from how utterly crushed he felt by the news of her engagement.

He didn't quite understand these feelings boring a hole into his chest. Jules was his friend. He should be happy for her, not feeling like he'd just lost his best friend.

She must've seen through his bravado because she put a hand on his arm.

"I'm only kidding. Sort of."

He gave his head a shake.

"I am so not following you. Are you engaged or not?"

"It's kind of a funny story, actually."

She told him about what had transpired during lunch with Helen at Le Marais—about the health bombshell her mom had dropped while they were eating lunch.

"First, she was overwrought about dying and leaving me alone in the world."

Jules told him about the little white lie she'd told that she wasn't *that far* away from getting married and how things had begun to spiral.

"I really thought telling her I was in a serious relationship with someone would make her feel better. Who knows, maybe when I get back to LA, I might actually meet someone and fall in love, but I'm digressing. After lunch, I went to Primrose Bridal to pick up my bridesmaid dress. While we were there, I let Mom goad me into trying on a wedding dress."

He raised his brows. "She goaded you? I thought that wasn't possible. I thought you were goad proof."

"Right? Well, Mom made a big deal about wanting to see me in a wedding dress. She said she wanted to see what I'd look like as a bride while she could still remember it. She wanted to see me in a dress, and I didn't have the heart to say no."

Owen shrugged. "Yeah, you were definitely goaded."

She held up a finger. "And it gets worse. I was standing there in that big white dress, and who do you suppose chose that precise moment to walk into the shop and pick up her dress for the wedding?"

"I have no idea."

"Kimmy Ogilvie."

He frowned in solidarity. "That's right. She's in the wedding, too, isn't she?"

Jules nodded. "She saw me in the bridal gown and immediately started showing off her big, fat engagement ring. Did you know she's engaged?"

"No. I haven't talked to Kimmy in years."

"Well, when Mom saw Kimmy's ring, she told Kimmy I was engaged, too. So my 'sort of serious with someone' little white lie morphed into me being engaged to someone. I know I should've corrected her, but Mom looked so happy—I mean, happier than I'd seen her since I arrived. I couldn't bear to disappoint her. Especially in front of Kimmy. I was in that dress. How embarrassing is that? To be caught trying on a wedding gown when you're not even engaged.

"Now, here we are. Both Mom and Kimmy think I'm engaged, and I was too chicken to tell them the truth. Am I a horrible person?"

"I can think of a lot of things worse than letting a sick woman believe something that makes her happy," Owen said.

"I know. And after Kimmy walked in flashing her engagement ring, there was no turning back," Jules said. "I have no idea how I'm going to get out of this one without breaking my mother's heart. At first, I thought I could get through the weekend and pretend to call off the engagement after I got home. Now, I'm having major liar's remorse. What am I going to do, Owen? If she dies believing this lie I told her…"

She sighed and put her head in her hands.

"You didn't exactly lie to her. You...didn't correct her. You let her believe what she wanted to believe. And she's not going to die, Jules. So stop worrying about that."

She sat up and looked at him. Owen put his arm around her and pulled her close. He breathed in the floral scent of her shampoo.

"No, she's not going to die," echoed the nurse who had stood in the way of Jules following her mother into the treatment area earlier. "At least not today, if we have anything to do with it."

The nurse flashed a smile.

Owen and Jules stood up in unison.

"How is she doing?" Jules asked the nurse.

"She's resting comfortably."

"Do you know what's wrong?" Owen asked.

The nurse shook her head. "Not yet. We're sending her out for a bunch of tests, but that won't happen for a few minutes. Would you like to see her for a quick moment? One of you can pop in, but when I said quickly, I meant like a nanosecond. I think it would make her happy. She was asking for you."

Before Jules followed her back, the nurse said, "I know you two, don't I? I think we went to high school together."

Owen could see her name tag now. It said Patty Jones.

He and Jules introduced themselves.

"It's nice to see you again, Patty," said Jules. "I was

going to say something earlier, but you've been so busy today."

"You're not kidding, and I'm not finished yet. Come on. If you want to see her, we'd better get in there while we can."

Owen stayed in the waiting room while Jules went back.

Patty wasn't joking when she said the visit had to be quick. Jules was back in less than five minutes. She came back to the waiting area looking marginally relieved.

"How's she doing?" Owen asked.

"She's looking better. They've given her some oxygen and an IV drip. Now we wait."

She settled in on the vinyl loveseat.

"Now that she introduced herself, I remember Patty," Jules said. "I think she was a year younger than us, wasn't she? I didn't get a chance to chat with her."

"That must be why she looked familiar, but I couldn't place her in our grade," Owen said.

"It was nice of her to let me see Mom."

"Yeah, it was," Owen said.

A few hours later, after they'd caught up on each other's lives and made multiple inquiries about Helen, Patty reappeared.

"I'm leaving for the day, but I wanted to make sure you knew where to find your mom. She's on the fourth floor, room 426."

"Oh, no. They're admitting her?" Jules asked. "Is it bad?"

Patty's face transformed into what appeared to be

a practiced, benevolent smile. "I'm sorry, but I'm not at liberty to say. However, she is in a regular room—a private room." She paused and gave Jules a look that seemed meant to convey what she couldn't say. "Why don't you two go up and see her? Her doctor should be along shortly and will be able to tell you everything. I'll look in on her tomorrow. I have to run, but it was so good to see y'all."

Patty gave a quick wave of her hand before turning and disappearing through the double doors.

"Judging by what Patty just said, I think Mom's okay." Jules looked at him pleadingly, as if silently imploring him to agree with her.

"You'll have to talk to her doctor, of course, but it stands to reason that if her life was in danger they'd have her in critical care. Why don't you go up and be with her?"

"Do you want to come?"

"If you don't mind, I think I'll go. Call me later and I'll come back and take you home."

"I can get an Uber," she said. "That way you won't have to come back out. You've already been so wonderful and spent so much time here."

"No, call me and I'll come get you." He kissed Jules on the cheek and she leaned into him and rested her head on his chest as if it was a respite from all of her worries. His arms went around her and pulled her close. She felt good in his arms, and he realized he was relieved that she wasn't engaged to someone else. It wasn't fair for him to want her all to himself, but in the heat of the moment, he hadn't been feeling rational.

He pushed the perplexing thought aside and simply held her, losing himself in the nearness of her.

Then a voice sounded over the hospital's intercom system, startling him back to the present.

"I'll be waiting for your call," he said as he put some distance between them.

She made a face that suggested she might object, but then she said, "Thanks, Owen. What would I do without you?"

As they each turned and walked in separate directions—she toward the elevator and he toward the entrance—he found himself thinking he'd never want to put that theory to the test.

Chapter Two

Juliette rapped lightly on the door of room 426 and then pushed it open a crack so that she could peek inside. Her mother was lying on the bed with her eyes closed. She was hooked up to a host of beeping and blinking machines.

Wheel of Fortune was on the television.

"Come in." She turned her head toward the door, pulling her attention away from the program.

"Oh, Juliette, it's you. I thought they'd never let me see you."

"I know." Juliette walked over to the bed and kissed her mother on the forehead, then smoothed her gray bangs back into place. "But I'm here now. What's wrong? They wouldn't tell me anything."

"I guess this old ticker of mine is acting up," she said.

"Did you have a heart attack?"

"I don't think so. I'm not sure. All I know is they performed just about every test in the book on me and they said I have a slow heart, which is exactly what the doctor told me when he diagnosed me with bradycardia. They'll have to give you the details. Something about installing a cardiac pacing device. Is that a pacemaker? They were talking so fast, I only caught about every other word they said."

Helen shrugged and looked back at the television.

"The phrase is *Fresh Baked Bread*. How can you not know that?" she said to the television and then turned back to Juliette. "How can they not know that? I should go on that show. I'd solve every single one of those puzzles. Come on, man! Choose the letter *b*. No, not *f*, the letter *b*. What is wrong with you? In what world does the letter *f* make sense in that sentence?"

"Mom, settle down. It's just a game show. There's no need to get upset over it."

"I'm not upset. I'm outraged. That's what I am. Once I'm all patched up and out of here, I'm going to apply to be a contestant on that program. I'll show them how it's done."

Helen's face fell. "That is, *if* I get out of here."

"Mom! Don't talk like that. Of course you're going to get out of here. You need to think positively and do what the doctor says."

"I don't know, Juliette. It seems like every day there's something else wrong with me, but I worry about you more than I worry about me. I want to meet that fellow of yours. I need to make sure that he's going to treat you right. I just need to know that you're going to be okay. Of course, going to your wedding, seeing my baby walk down the aisle, is a reason to live. And then there would be grandkids. I guess you'll start trying to get pregnant right away? I mean, you're thirty years old. You don't have any time to lose."

Actually, she'd turned thirty-one a few months ago. Her mom had forgotten her birthday, but Juliette had been on location and had been so busy she'd nearly forgotten it herself.

Should her mom forgetting her birthday have been a sign that something was wrong? She hadn't said anything because she hadn't wanted to seem like a big baby about it, but now she was second-guessing her decision.

She would mention it to the doctor first chance she got.

Right on cue, a woman in a lab coat carrying a tablet knocked on the door and walked in.

"Good evening, Helen. I'm Dr. Strand. It looks like they put you through the ringer today with all those stress tests. How are you feeling?"

"Exhausted," Helen said. "This is my daughter, Juliette."

"Nice to meet you," said the doctor. "Is it okay if I speak in front of Juliette?"

"Absolutely," Helen said. "She's my next of kin and my medical power of attorney. It's important that she hears everything you have to say."

"Of course," said the doctor. "Let me wash my hands and we'll get down to business."

She performed a quick checkup, listening to Helen's heart and looking at her records.

"The good news is you did not have a heart attack," said Dr. Strand. "The news that could be better is based on the tests we performed today and the Holter monitor that your primary care doctor prescribed—it seems you have a sluggish heart. I'm happy to say we should be able to correct your problem with a pacemaker, if you're willing. It should make you feel much better."

"Honestly, I'd do just about anything to feel better, Doctor," said Helen. "What's involved?"

Dr. Strand went through the procedure.

"We're keeping you overnight for observation," said the doctor. "Since you're here, I could perform the procedure tomorrow, if you'd like. Or if you'd rather think about it, we can schedule it for a later date. It's up to you, but I would suggest the sooner, the better."

Helen looked at Juliette. "I hate to do this while you're visiting."

"Do you not live in town?"

"I live in LA," Juliette said. "But Mom, I'm between projects right now. I can stay a little longer if you need me."

Helen's face brightened. "Will your fiancé be okay without you?" She turned to the doctor. "My daughter is engaged to be married. I'm so proud."

Juliette clasped her right hand over her left to cover her bare ring finger. Then she mentally berated herself for being so foolish. Not everyone wore an engagement ring. Besides, the doctor's attention was trained on her tablet, not on Juliette's jewelry—or lack thereof.

"Is there anyone else in the house with you, Helen?" the doctor asked.

"It's just me. My husband passed several years ago. Juliette gets here when she can, but she's so busy. She works in film."

"I can tell you're very proud of her. However, you'll need someone to help you for about a month to six weeks after the procedure. You should start feeling better immediately, but there will be some limitations while your body heals and gets used to the device. So, if your daughter can't be there, you'll want to find someone who can."

"I'll be there, Mom."

"Maybe your young man can visit you while you're here." Helen sounded almost giddy. "Then I could meet him."

Heat bloomed on Juliette's cheeks, and suddenly the room felt like a greenhouse. "Mom, we can talk about that later. Right now, we need to focus on you and getting you prepared for your procedure tomorrow."

"Of course, dear." Helen winked at Juliette.

As the doctor wrapped up her visit, a food service worker delivered Helen's dinner.

Juliette took that opportunity to follow the doctor out into the hall.

"Dr. Strand, if you have a moment, there's something else I'd like to ask you about."

Juliette told the doctor about her mother's memory problems. She stopped short of getting into the misunderstanding over the engagement, but she managed to voice her concerns.

"Your mom's condition can cause confusion and even memory loss. And is she taking a statin?" The doctor checked her tablet and then tapped on it with her short, manicured fingernail. "I see here that she is. That can exacerbate the problem. It's definitely worth mentioning to her primary care doctor, but in the meantime, I'd suggest that we take it one step at a time. Let's see what kind of improvement she experiences after tomorrow's procedure, and we'll take it from there."

Maybe this unexpected break between projects was meant to be. At least she didn't have to cancel or cut out of a film early. She was free and clear to stay in town. Back in her old bedroom.

Back to square one.

But this was no time to feel sorry for herself. She was grateful for the opportunity to help her mom.

As she pushed open the door to her mom's hospital room, she wondered what Owen was doing. It was so good of him to offer to come back and pick her up. She'd need to call him and tell him she would be staying with her mom tonight.

Just knowing that he was there, that she could lean on him, made everything seem a lot easier.

It had been the day from hell, Owen thought as he collapsed onto the steering wheel of his car.

First, Helen Kingsbury had landed in the emergency room. Next, when he'd gotten home from the hospital, Dan Richter, the investor Owen had thought was a sure thing, called to deliver the crushing news that he was having second thoughts about investing in Owen's smart home tech startup. Owen had been working tirelessly for months trying to find a venture capital group or individual to invest. After a lot of noes, Richter had seemed so promising.

Until Richter binge-watched the latest season of *Selling Sandcastle,* the reality television show that followed Owen and his family. Post-binge, Richter had decided he wasn't completely comfortable with how Owen had presented himself.

For the past three seasons, *Selling Sandcastle* had chronicled the ins and outs of the coastal North Carolina beachfront real estate market by filming the goings on at Sandcastle Real Estate, the business Bert McFadden and Barbara "Bunny" Bradshaw McFadden had started more than fifteen years ago.

In each of the three seasons the show had aired, the producer, Dalton Hart, had made one person look like a villain.

Last year, he'd framed Owen.

"Frankly, it wasn't a good look, McFadden," Richter had said. "I need to know that you're all in on this company you want me to sink money into. The guy I saw on the show seemed more interested in catching waves, getting tan and mugging for the television cameras. This project you've proposed will take a lot of time and effort to get off the ground. I don't see how you're going to find that focus if you're going in a bunch of different directions. More than that, I'm afraid that you're going to get bored before you see this project through. Your smart home idea is good, but I'm not convinced you'll stick with it long enough to get it from point A to point B."

It took some fast-talking, but Owen had managed to convince Richter to give him a chance to prove who he was, that the guy portrayed on the reality television show was a product of editing and a plan to make him look like a vapid slacker. The thing that clinched things

was Owen telling him that, because of how he was portrayed, he'd bowed out of being on the show this season.

"That's not me," he'd said. "I hope you'll give me a
chance to show you just how serious I am about Smart-
Scape Technologies."

Five minutes after he'd hung up with Richter, a group
text from his father to Owen and his siblings—Logan,
Forest and Sophie—came through, asking when they
could all get together for a family meeting. He and their
mother had something important to discuss with them.
He wouldn't tell them what they wanted to talk about,
but had said sooner would be better than later.

After the day Owen had had, all he could think was
what now?

After a bit of back and forth, they'd agreed to meet
later that evening. That time worked best for everyone. Probably because curiosity had gotten the best of
them—why else would they agree to meet at 10:30 p.m.?

He might have to leave early if Jules needed a ride
home… It was curious that she hadn't texted by now.
He would've thought that visiting hours would be over.

He dashed off a quick text to her.

Your car awaits. Let me know if you need a ride. Happy
to pick you up.

Exiting his car, he looked around the expansive circular driveway to see that he had been the first to ar-
rive. In fact, even his parents weren't home yet. He let
himself into the large, oceanfront home.

Without his family there, the big house was eerily

quiet, except for the echo of his footsteps as he made his way toward the kitchen.

When he flipped the light on, he spied a covered glass cake plate laden with chocolate chip cookies that his mom had set out on the kitchen island. He lifted the dome and helped himself to one of the treats. A single bite confirmed that they were so fresh and delicious that she must have baked them earlier that day.

His mom was pretty amazing. After beating breast cancer, she'd made the decision to take a step back from the family real estate business to do the things she loved, such as baking and volunteering in the community. In that sense, she'd become an ambassador for Sandcastle Real Estate, relishing the opportunity to represent the company while giving back to the Tinsley Cove community.

A leaden weight of dread pushed down as it occurred to him that this meeting might be about his mother's health. Had she relapsed? Was that the reason for the family meeting? So they could break the news to everyone all at once?

He brushed the thought aside. There was no sense in worrying until he knew for sure.

Tonight, their parents had hosted an awards dinner honoring the employees of Sandcastle Real Estate.

Business had never been better. The show *Selling Sandcastle* had given the business such exposure that real estate sales were off the charts. The good sales meant opportunities for the McFaddens to expand Sandcastle Real Estate into larger markets and take on agents outside of the family—a big step for a family-owned-and-operated business.

Aside from the obvious monetary perks, another bright side of the expansion had been that it had made it easier for Owen to step away from Sandcastle Real Estate without creating even as much as a ripple in sales or the production of the television show. There had been dozens of agents ready to step in. And since Owen's heart had never been in sales—he was wired for technology—the hungry go-getters had more than made up for the numbers he'd produced.

Even so, his leaving Sandcastle Real Estate hadn't come without a certain amount of angst. His brother Logan had moved back to Tinsley Cove after their mother's health scare. After Bunny had healed, she'd been ecstatic to not only have her four children back in the same town, but also to have them all working for the family business.

But real estate simply wasn't his passion. He'd always wanted his own business in technology. More than that, he wanted to be his own boss. During COVID lockdown, when real estate showings had been at an all-time low, he'd taken steps toward that end.

That's why now Owen had a secret that he hadn't confided in anyone close to him.

Not even Jules.

During lockdown, he had created a browser-based word video game called *Phrase Fusion*. It had become all the rage over the past few months, after he had sold it to a national news organization—for a lot of money. When the news organization had approached him last year, he'd quietly set up an LLC called RomeO Enterprises. It was the first name that popped into his head.

While the had gained a cult following before the news organization had acquired it, after the game appeared on the paper's app and website a couple of months ago, no one had questioned its origin or creator, other than attributing it to a small startup called RomeO Enterprises.

Not even his family or Jules or other friends knew he was behind it. He hadn't told any of them about it because his subsequent attempts at creating other games hadn't landed as successfully as *Phrase Fusion*. He hated the feeling of being a one-hit wonder. Because even though he'd received a hefty sum from the sale, it wasn't enough to make him independently wealthy. However, it was enough to allow him to leave the real estate business and still have a means to support himself, and he was able to focus on another tech project he'd been interested in: smart home technology.

Shortly after his family had purchased the house his parents now called home, a group of thugs had subverted the house's basic security system, broken in and trashed the place. The only saving grace was that none of their family had been there when it had happened and they hadn't moved in many of their belongings.

It could've been so much worse, but even all these years later, Owen was still haunted by the what-ifs of that fateful day. That's how he'd become interested in smart home safety and technology.

That was the reason he'd gone all-or-nothing and invested most of the money he'd made off of *Phrase Fusion* into his new smart home technology venture.

Dan Richter's investment was supposed to help Owen bring it all home and make it a reality. Without Richter's cash, Owen stood to lose everything he'd put into it.

Technology changed so rapidly. That's why this had to happen *now*.

Plus, it would be the sustainable win he so desperately needed. Then he would tell his family and others about *Phrase Fusion*. What others had viewed as creative dalliances would be vindicated. Rather than writing him off as the dilettante and the dreamer, they'd finally see him as a success.

He had a unique idea for a smart home technology startup.

Going beyond the usual smart home systems that controlled locks, televisions, thermostats, appliances and home security systems, SmartScape Technologies integrated advanced image processing that could analyze gestures, posture and gait for enhanced security. When activated, certain settings in the unique system Owen had designed could discern between who was welcome in a dwelling and an uninvited intruder, improving the homeowners' safety and security.

For a long time Owen had wished something like that had been available before his parents' place had been ransacked. It wasn't. So he created it.

The marketplace needed this.

Now he needed to convince Dan Richter of that fact.

He needed to prove to him he was not the unmotivated loser that he had appeared to be in last season's *Selling Sandcastle*. That was compliments of Dalton Hart's editing. Every season had a villain. Last season,

Hart had zeroed in on Owen, making it appear that all he did was play video games and surf all day.

Why hadn't he simply announced that he was the mastermind behind *Phrase Fusion*? Because while it had gained a cult following, it wasn't the sensation it was now until the news organization had acquired it.

The acquisition didn't happen overnight, and in the months between being approached and signing on the dotted line, Owen hadn't been at liberty to talk about it. Especially not on a reality television show.

It is what it is, he thought as he plucked another cookie off the plate and bit into its chewy goodness.

Rather than sulking about it—or eating his feelings—he needed to figure out a plan B or, better yet, a way to convince Richter to change his mind.

"Hey, save some for us," Logan said as he and his wife, Cassie, walked into the kitchen.

"You snooze, you lose," Owen said. "I was here on time."

"Sorry, it was my fault." Cassie walked over and hugged Owen. "I got home late and then I had to walk Luna. It's been a crazy day."

Luna was Cassie's Pembroke Welsh corgi.

"I hear you," he said. "Must be in the air. Any idea what this meeting is about?"

"We were wondering the same thing," Logan said.

"Is Mom all right?" Owen asked.

"As far as we know," Logan said. He and Cassie shot him questioning, concerned looks, but he waved away the nonverbal inquiry.

His sister walked in with their oldest brother, Forest, and his wife, Avery.

"What about Mom?" asked Sophie.

"She and Dad aren't here yet, but she left us some damn good cookies," said Owen.

As his siblings swarmed around the cookies, Jules's text came through.

Jules: I meant to text you earlier, but I've been focusing on my mom. Thanks for offering to pick me up, but I've decided to stay at the hospital with her tonight. She's doing well and will feel even better after having a minor procedure tomorrow.

Owen: Give your mom my best. I'll bring breakfast in the morning.

Jules: You're the best.

Owen: Isn't that why you keep me around? Sleep well.

He had just pushed Send on his reply when his father walked in holding his tie and unbuttoning the top buttons of his white shirt.

"Hello, everyone," said Bert.

"Sorry we're late," Bunny said, trailing in behind him, wearing a black beaded cocktail dress. She slipped out of her heels and set them out of the way of foot traffic. "It went a bit longer than we anticipated. Of course, since we were hosting, we couldn't leave until everyone else did. I'm glad you found the cookies. By the way, Owen, several people were saying that Helen Kingsbury had a medical emergency this afternoon. Is Juliette home yet? I know she's in the wedding."

True to form, news traveled fast in Tinsley Cove. He wondered if questions about Jules's "engagement" would follow. After all, she had been seen trying on a bridal gown, and Jules hadn't corrected Helen when she'd told Kimmy Ogilvie that Jules was engaged.

Just about the only thing that could preempt that juicy morsel of gossip was Helen landing in the emergency room.

Owen nodded. "Yes, she got in earlier today. I happened to drive by when Helen was having her episode, and I ended up driving her and Jules to the hospital."

"Is Helen okay?" Bert asked.

"I think so. Jules just texted me and said they were keeping her overnight because she was having some sort of procedure tomorrow morning. She wasn't specific, and I didn't think it was appropriate to ask for details over text. Jules is staying with her at the hospital tonight. I'm going to drop by tomorrow."

"I'm so sorry to hear that," Bunny said. "I hope she'll be okay. Let me know if there's anything we can do. Be sure to take her some flowers when you go to the hospital. But you might want to call and make sure she can have flowers. Some floors don't allow them, depending on what's wrong with the patient."

"Good idea," Owen said. "I'll call the nurses' station first thing and check."

With that, silence fell over the room. His parents exchanged a look, and he had a feeling that something was up. Wasn't bad news supposed to come in threes?

If so, was this number three in the set that included Helen's trip to emergency and Dan Richter's cold feet?

"Is everything okay?" Forest asked

They exchanged another look, clearly communicating in that silent language in which married couples became fluent after spending most of their lives together.

"Why don't we all go into the living room," Bert suggested.

After everyone had claimed a seat, Bert remained standing. Bunny sat down on the couch between Owen and Sophie. His parents looked so somber that Owen braced himself for the worst news.

Again, the question crossed his mind: had his mother's cancer returned? If not, was his father's health failing?

Since his mother's diagnosis, the couple had prided themselves on healthy living, but they were in their mid-seventies. A person could do everything right, but nobody lived forever.

Owen swallowed the fear-driven bile that was churning in the back of his throat and resolved to let them speak first.

Finally, his father said, "There's a couple of things we need to tell you." He cleared his throat and jingled the change in his pocket. "First, your mother and I have decided to follow Owen's lead. This will be our last season of *Selling Sandcastle*. I hope you're not upset that we didn't consult you before we made the decision, but we thought it was best to leave while we were still having fun. You're welcome to talk to Dalton about continuing the show or coming up with some sort of spin-off."

Dalton Hart was the owner of Top Drawer Productions and the executive producer of *Selling Sandcastle*.

Owen blinked and digested what his father had just said. That wasn't so bad. He had opted out of the fourth season because Hart had made him look like an idiot. The show ending was no skin off his nose, though his brothers, their wives and Sophie were still actively involved.

"Are you both okay, health-wise?" he asked, wanting to cut to the chase.

"Oh, why, yes." Bunny sounded surprised by the question. "We've never been better. In fact, that's part of the reason that we've decided…" She glanced at Bert. "I'll let your father fill you in since he's doing such a good job."

Bert smiled at her. "You're perfectly welcome to tell them if you'd like."

They did that silent communication thing again. Only, this time, it was more like silent flirting.

"I don't care which one of you tells us," Sophie said. "But I would like to know what was so important that we had to have a family meeting at ten thirty at night."

"The only reason it had to be at this hour is because this was the only time that worked for everyone," Bert said. "Your mom and I appreciate you making the time to come over here. I know everyone is busy. That's why it was difficult to coordinate eight schedules. I know it's late, so I'll cut to the chase.

"Your mom and I have decided to slow down a bit and enjoy ourselves. We've worked nearly every waking hour over the past decade and a half, and we've decided it's time to retire and sell the house. Since we're empty nesters and you all have lives of your own, there's no sense in hanging on to it. We would like to downsize into a lock-it-and-leave-it sort of place, which will make it much easier for us to travel. We all know firsthand how fragile health can be and, well, we want to get away from the limelight, and the office for that matter, while we still are well enough to travel."

His siblings and their spouses murmured their surprise, but all in all, they were supportive.

"We will need to get the house show ready," said Bunny. "What that means is you'll need to get anything you've been storing here over the years—sports trophies, old yearbooks, out-of-style wardrobes and all the various and sundries that you've been collecting."

This time, the siblings sounded a collective moan. It was such a large house that they'd each had their own bedroom when they'd lived there. Their parents had kept the rooms mostly the same as when the kids had occupied them. Owen knew that he still had boxes of old mementos that he'd need to remove from the house so that potential buyers could open closets and not see the clutter.

"If you would rather, we could just take care of it for you," Bert said. "But be warned that we won't be able to take it to our new place. We won't have room."

The consensus seemed to be that each person would come over and go through their old rooms and decide what to keep and what to toss.

Just when the lead ball in the pit of Owen's stomach

was starting to lighten, Bert and Bunny exchanged another one of their looks.

"What?" Owen asked. "Is there something else?"

"There's the matter of the business," Bert said. "Since we'll be away, we'd like for Forest, Logan and Sophie to run the daily operations of Sandcastle Real Estate."

The pause that followed was so heavy that Owen wondered if he'd missed something, but then he felt the gazes of his siblings on him.

"That makes sense," he said.

His parents seemed to exhale in unison.

"You're okay with that, Owen?" his mother asked.

"Of course. Why wouldn't I be?"

"Well, Sandcastle is a family-owned-and-operated business, and you were a valuable part of it," Bunny said. "We understand why you wanted to do your own thing, but your father and I just wanted to make sure that you didn't feel like you were being shut out."

"Mom, it was my decision to leave," Owen said. "Real estate sales was never my forte."

"We want you to know," said his father, "that if you ever change your mind and want to get back into the business, there's a place for you."

Owen smiled. "Thank you. I really appreciate it."

"You had mentioned that you'd hear something soon about the silent partner who was interested in investing in your idea. Any news?" All eyes were on him, and he couldn't bring himself to say that something that had looked so promising might be imploding. His family members—every single one of them—were so successful. Giving credit where credit was due, they worked hard, but sometimes it seemed like success came easily to them.

Right now, he felt as if he had to claw his way to every minute gain.

"I'll let you know as soon as I have something to report."

Bunny clapped her hands. "Owen, your father and I are so proud of you. We're proud of all of our kids. We always knew you'd be successful in whatever you chose to do with your lives. Just look at you all. Our family has grown with Logan and Forest marrying Cassie and Avery. I'm longing for the day that you bless us with grandchildren."

The married couples shifted and grinned at their spouses. For a moment, Owen wondered if one of them might make an announcement to that end, but no one seized the moment.

"As Owen so aptly put it," Logan said, "we'll let you know as soon as we have something to report."

Bunny beamed at them. "We are so very blessed to be such a close family. The way we support each other is more valuable than all the fame and money in the world. Owen, as soon as everything is in place, we will celebrate your success."

Owen shrugged. "It's a little premature to think about celebrating, but it's good to think positive."

The next morning, Owen called the nurses' station on the fourth floor and learned that Helen could, indeed, have flowers.

The nurse who answered said, "I don't see why not.

After the way she was poked and prodded yesterday, it will probably be a nice treat for her."

Owen thanked the nurse and headed out to Daisy's Flower Emporium to pick up a bouquet of mixed flowers. He stopped by the bakery for bagels and coffee and then headed to the hospital.

Bringing Helen flowers this morning and a couple of bagels for her and Jules was an opportunity to do something nice for her. After all, Helen Kingsbury had been like a second mother to him when he was growing up. Owen and his family had lived next door to Jules's family for years until Owen's parents had gotten their big break in real estate.

Owen had been starting high school when his parents had moved the family into the larger house where he and his family had met last night. It was about a mile down Tinsley Cove Beach. His parents' new-found wealth and the big, fancy house—and the doors their success had opened around town—had meant new friend groups for Owen, too.

Suddenly, everyone had wanted to be his friend, popular kids, like Kimmy Ogilvie and her ilk, who hadn't given him the time of day before he'd moved into the right neighborhood.

Even so, after the move, Owen had chosen to hang out at Jules's house every chance he got. Even though the place was modest and Jules wasn't part of his new group of friends, hanging out with her at her house felt more like coming home than living in the rambling beachfront mansion his folks still called home today.

He didn't begrudge his parents the house of their dreams. It had just never felt like home to him.

When he stepped out of the elevator and into the main hall of the fourth floor, the first person he saw was Jules walking toward him. "Look at you, Sleeping Beauty," he said.

She bent her arms at the elbow and held up her hands, palms up, and struck a pose. "Don't judge. I haven't had my coffee yet. I was just heading out to find some." She gestured to the paper bag and cardboard drinks tray he was holding. "If that's what I think it is, I will love you forever."

"Okay, you're committed," he said and held out the tray of coffee so she could take it.

"Those are pretty." She nodded at the flowers.

"I figured Helen could use some cheering up."

"She's not too bad off since she found out I'll be staying for at least a month to help her out after her procedure."

Owen's eyes went wide. "You will? I mean, can you get away for that long?"

Jules nodded.

"Of course you can. Knowing you, even if it wasn't convenient, I know you'd find a way to make it work."

She smiled at him. "You got here just in time. They're prepping her for the procedure now. She can't eat anything, but I'm sure she'll be starving after everything is finished."

"If now's not a good time, I can come back later," he said. "My being here might make it too chaotic. I understand if you want some time alone with her."

"Are you kidding?" Jules said. "I just spent all night with her, Owen. She'd probably rather see you than me. You always were her favorite."

Owen smiled. "Okay, I'll take that."

"At least poke your head in and say hello. I know she'll be so happy to see you. Then you can keep me company while I wait. Unless you have something else to do."

"I'm wide open this morning. This afternoon, I need to help Jack with some things."

Jules gasped. "That reminds me. I need to get in touch with Tasha and tell her what's happened. I hate to add to a bride's angst, but if Mom needs me, I might have to miss some of the pre-wedding events. I'll have to reach out to my roommates, Ingrid and Harry, too, in case I have to extend my stay."

"Do you think you'll be able to make the wedding this weekend?"

"I should be able to, but maybe I should wait and see how Mom is doing. I hate to leave Tasha hanging, but…" She trailed off, and for the first time, Owen realized that she looked downright scared.

"I'm sure Natasha will understand and support you with whatever you need to do," Owen said.

Then they walked in silence down the hall and stopped in front of Helen's room.

"Listen," Owen said. "I'm here for you. You don't have to go through this alone."

He pulled her into a hug.

They were still embracing when the door to Helen's room opened. An orderly was wheeling Helen out on a gurney.

Owen and Jules turned to her. Owen left his arm around Jules's shoulder.

"I didn't realize you were taking her down so soon," Jules said. "I would've never left the room if I'd known."

"No worries," said Patty Jones, the nurse they'd talked to last night. She was standing at the head of Helen's gurney. "We're not putting her out for this procedure. It only requires a local anesthetic to numb the area, but we need to get that started as soon as possible. I've already given her a sedative to relax her."

A groggy-looking Helen opened her eyes. "Juliette, is that you?"

"Yes, I'm here, Mom. Everything is going to be okay. Just relax, and the next thing you know, it will all be over and you'll be as good as new."

"Is that Owen with you?" Helen asked.

Owen bent down to Helen's level. "Yes, ma'am. It's me. I brought you some flowers. We'll put them in water while you're getting all fixed up."

"That's so sweet of you," Helen said, slurring her words. "Nurse Patty, this is Owen McFadden, my daughter's fiancé."

"Oh, Mom, no. This is just Owen."

"That's what I said." Helen's eyes drooped. "I always wanted you two to get married. You've made me the happiest mama in the world because I know I can count on you, Owen, to take good care of my Juliette after I'm gone. Now I don't have to worry about her anymore."

Owen watched Juliette open her mouth to set the record straight, but before she could, the nurse said, "Okay, Mrs. Kingsbury, we need to be on our way now.

You have a date with Dr. Strand, and we don't want to keep her waiting." Patty turned to Juliette and Owen. "I'll let you know when she's in recovery. Congratulations, you two. Even in high school, I always thought you two would end up together."

As Owen digested Patty's words, he realized the idea didn't make him want to run. Maybe the woman was onto something.

At least for the time being.

Chapter Three

"Patty, do you have a moment?" Juliette asked.

Patty glanced at the gurney as if she might refuse the request. Then she motioned for the orderly to continue. "I'll catch up with you in a second, Fred."

"I just wanted to set the record straight," Juliette said. "I think my mother's condition has her a bit confused, which is something I'd like to discuss with the doctor."

"Confusion is not unusual with bradycardia, which is your mother's diagnosis. With the pacemaker, it should correct itself. Don't worry. The doctor can tell you more when she checks in after your mother's procedure."

"That's good to know," Juliette said before Patty could get away. "But just to set the record straight, Owen and I are good friends, but we're not engaged. I think that was just my mother's wishful thinking."

"Oh, well, okay." Patty glanced at Owen, then back at Juliette. "It wasn't such a stretch to think you two would end up together, but if not—" Patty shrugged as if she wanted to say, *No biggie*, but was too polite to vocalize.

Juliette watched as the nurse quickened her pace to catch up with Helen's gurney, and for a fraction of a second, she regretted telling Patty the truth.

Patty had believed they were truly in love and preparing to spend the rest of their lives together.

For a moment, Juliette let her mind indulge in the fantasy of being engaged to Owen. A montage of them falling in love, him proposing and putting a ring on her finger and them waking up together in the same bed every day for the rest of their lives made goose bumps form along her spine. Their happily ever after swirled through her mind as if her life were flashing before her eyes.

And she didn't hate it.

In fact, it made her feel a little weak in the knees and fluttery in her belly, but she'd done the right thing by setting the record straight.

"That was awkward." She stared down at the tray of cups she was holding for a moment because she was afraid that if she looked at him, he might see through her, straight to what she'd been thinking.

"Actually, it *was* kind of weird."

"What do you mean?" she asked, warily.

"Neither one of us remembered Patty's name. Yet she not only remembered us, but she also thought we'd end up together?"

Juliette was tempted to ask him if the idea was really that unpalatable, because it hadn't seemed like it the night he'd suggested they be each other's default life partners in case they found themselves thirty and still single.

And here they were, exactly that.

Except Owen seemed to be completely fine with being footloose and fancy-free. It's not that she wasn't fine with it, but it was interesting how easily she had slipped into the role of fiancée in her mind.

She fidgeted with the hem of her blouse, pulling at it as if getting it to lie just right would make this unsettled feeling go away.

"You know how it was. The lowerclassmen always looked up to the upperclassmen, but the upperclassmen were usually so focused on getting out of high school, they were oblivious to everyone else. I did the right thing by telling her, didn't I?"

Owen shrugged. "I guess so."

She grimaced. "It just hit me that confessing to Patty might have blown my cover with my mom and with Kimmy Ogilvie." She shrugged. "What Kimmy thinks is the least of my concerns right now. But if my mom wakes up still believing we're engaged, I'd like to be the one who tells her the truth. I hope Patty doesn't say anything to her. Maybe I should talk to Patty and ask her not to say anything."

"I think Patty is a little busy right now," Owen said.

"I know," Juliette said. "I didn't mean we should hunt her down right this second, but when I see her again I should tell her what happened."

Owen had a weird look on his face. "Yeah, about that…" The way he was looking at her made her stomach bunch and flip.

"What?" she asked, resisting the urge to pull on her blouse again. It was a bad habit that she needed to stop.

"Your mom is going to be in there for a while," he said. "Why don't we ask one of the nurses if she can put these flowers in some water, then let's go somewhere we can talk privately?"

Privately? Why?

What more was there to say?

Juliette glanced around to see who might overhear them. Most of the hospital room doors were shut, but a few were open a crack and a couple of nurses were at the station, which was located about twenty yards away from where they stood.

"Why don't we just go in here?" Juliette hooked a thumb in the direction of her mom's room.

Owen nodded, but then he pointed to the tray of cups that Juliette was holding. "The coffee is probably cold. Why don't we go to the cafeteria and see if we can warm these up? We could hang out there for a bit, eat our bagels and talk before we come back here to wait for her. The change of scenery would probably do you some good since you were in that room all night."

"What do you want to talk about?" she asked. "Should I be scared?"

Owen's gaze searched her face, and she was aware that she hadn't showered or brushed her hair since yesterday. Thank goodness she'd washed her face and Patty had found her a toothbrush and some toothpaste.

"I have a proposal for you," he said.

She started to say, *Isn't a proposal what got us into trouble in the first place? Or at least my mom imagining you'd proposed.*

Instead, she nodded and fell into stride beside him, holding on to the coffee tray and the small white paper bag with the bagels as if they were a lifeline.

After Owen handed off the flowers to a nurse, he said. "Let me carry the tray."

He'd swept it out of her hands before she could protest, leaving her with the bag containing the bagels.

They found their way to the cafeteria and warmed their coffees in a microwave oven that was perched on a table between soda and snack vending machines. The place wasn't very busy—probably because they were between the breakfast and lunch rushes—if there were such things. Still, they chose a table nestled in a private corner away from the handful of people in the place.

She forced herself to wait until they both had a bagel in front of them, unwrapped and resting on the red-and-white-checked deli paper spread on the table, before she said, "Okay, spill it. What's so important that you needed to talk to me in private, Owen?"

Of course, he had just taken a bite of his bagel. He held up a finger as he chewed, giving the international sign for not wanting to talk with his mouth full. His good manners were one of the many things she loved about him.

But in the span of time between chewing and speaking, Juliette had a sudden panicked thought. What if Owen had met someone? What if he wanted to tell her that they always had been and always would be the best of *friends*, but he'd finally fallen in love with someone?

It was ridiculous, but she had to hold her breath for a few beats to stave off the stinging sensation that needled the backs of her eyes as she stared down at her untouched everything bagel with light vegetable cream cheese. Just the way she liked it. No matter how long it had been since they'd last seen each other, Owen always remembered the little things like this.

Because he was such a good…friend.

He would, no doubt, make some lucky woman a great husband.

It just wouldn't be her.

"Okay, hear me out before you say anything," he said as he dragged a paper napkin over his mouth.

She inhaled a sharp breath of antiseptic-smelling air, then looked up at him straight into his earnest green eyes. Eyes that had always touched her all the way down to her soul.

She nodded, relieved that she'd been stronger than the urge to cry that had gripped her a moment ago.

"Maybe an engagement ruse isn't such a crazy thing."

He scrubbed his hand over his chin and that fabulous square jawline of his.

She blinked to get her mind back on what he was saying. "What do you mean?"

Her heart pounded as she reminded herself that the operative word here was *ruse: a deception, a scam, a plot, a hoax.*

But what did that have to do with her? With them?

"I mean, since your mom believes we're engaged—"

"Owen, that was the drugs they'd given her talking. Or her medical condition. She's not herself right now."

"Okay, but she believes you're engaged. You didn't tell her you were engaged to anyone in particular, yet she believes I'm your fiancé."

"But we're not really engaged," Juliette said. "I just very awkwardly set the record straight with Patty Jones."

"We don't run in the same circles as Patty Jones," he reminded her. "In fact, we didn't even remember her until she introduced herself, and I still wouldn't swear I've met her before or that we have any friends in common. Just because she's your mom's nurse today, doesn't mean we'll run into her again outside of the hospital. I mean, when was the last time you set foot in this place?"

"I don't live in Tinsley Cove anymore, Owen."

"I know you don't, but I do and I have never been here until yesterday, and I haven't run into Patty Jones anywhere else."

"Maybe you have, but you just didn't remember who she was?"

"That's beside the point. Patty said that it wasn't so farfetched that we would end up together. What's to say that I didn't propose to you right after she walked away? Like this—Juliette Kingsbury, will you pretend to be engaged to me?" he said.

Her cheeks flamed, and she was sure she was as red as the blouse she was wearing. "What? Why?"

She glanced around, newly aware of why he wanted to talk privately.

"Owen, why do you want us to pretend to be engaged? That makes no sense."

More than being afraid that people would overhear her, she feared that she was as transparent as a fish tank and he could read every thought and feeling swimming through her mind and body. Such as the way her mind was screaming, *I don't care about the reason. YES! I'll pretend to be engaged to you.* And her heart was feeling all squishy and making her think crazy things like wanting to ask him, *Why don't we actually get married instead of pretending? Remember the thirty-thirty agreement?*

Luckily, her very thin skin was keeping all these thoughts inside—even though she felt all tingly, as if she were about to rip open at the seams and everything was about to spill out.

"Like I said before, hear me out before you say no."

He looked at her. She raised her eyebrows at him and made a circular motion with her hand that suggested he should get on with it.

"You know that smart home project I've been working on?"

Juliette nodded.

"I thought I had financing lined up," he said. "It seemed like a done deal, until the investor took issue with the fact that I'm, uh—"

He sucked in a breath and rubbed the back of his neck.

"He hasn't said no. Not in so many words, but he is hesitating because he thinks I might be a bad risk because of how I was portrayed on *Selling Sandcastle*."

"Wait, I don't understand."

"Last night, the investor—his name is Dan Richter, he's in California, in the Silicon Valley. He called and said he had just binge-watched the latest season of *Selling Sandcastle* and wasn't completely comfortable with how I had presented myself."

Owen shrugged.

"I agree that it wasn't a good look," Owen said.

"But that wasn't your fault. We both know that the producer had a storyline in mind and edited the footage to make you look like a flake."

Owen made a face at her. "Don't mince words, Jules."

"I said it wasn't your fault."

"Yeah, but the thing is, crying *not my fault* makes it seem like I'm playing the victim. That's not a good look, either. I agreed to be on the show. I knew what Hart was capable of, and I got burned."

He shrugged. "I need to prove to him that I'm all in on the smart home tech. That I'm more than the guy he saw on the show who was chilling out, catching waves and goofing off for the television cameras. My smart home project will take time and focus to get it off the ground. I need to prove to him that I'm grounded and committed, that I'm not going in a bunch of different directions."

"And you think you can change his mind if you suddenly turn up engaged?" Juliette asked.

Owen gave her a one-shoulder shrug. "Why not? Getting married shows an intent to settle down and be grounded. I'll have a family to support—or at least a wife. In theory."

"Won't it seem a little fishy that right after he said he thinks you're a flake, you turn up engaged? It doesn't take a rocket scientist to figure out what you're doing there, buddy. Aren't there other investors out there?"

"It's a tough market out there right now. I've been turned down by dozens of venture capitalists. It's not exactly like applying for a bank loan. At least for right now, he's my best prospect, especially if you look at the terms we've agreed to. He's not a hard no. I need to convince him that I am not that guy, and I think introducing him to my fiancée will turn him around."

She knew better than to suggest he ask his parents to finance the project, and she respected his need to do this on his own terms.

But still, there had to be a different way.

"I don't know, Owen. This sounds like a recipe for disaster to me. It's not honest."

He looked down at his hands. "I know, and that's the part I don't like. However, after SmartScape Technologies launches and Richter makes a lot of money, I believe he will forgive me the little white lie. In fact, once we're at that point, I'll confess."

Juliette looked down. "If we did pretend to be engaged, by the time you're rolling in dough, we will have called off the engagement, so it wouldn't really matter."

He nudged her foot under the table. When she didn't look up, he reached out, put a finger under her chin and gently lifted her head until she met his gaze.

"You're my oldest friend, Jules. I haven't been dating anyone else because I've been too busy trying to get my business off the ground to meet anyone. Think about it. It's not so unbelievable that our friendship turned into something more and we've been dating long-distance. Even Patty said as much.

"Besides, Dan Richter, the investor, was right there with the offer until *Selling Sandcastle* spooked him. He believes in what I'm doing."

"As long as you're married," Juliette said.

Owen shrugged. "As long as I'm engaged. I think that will prove to him that I'm more grounded than he thinks."

He took her hand in his, and her stomach flipped.

"And then what? What happens when you call off your engagement that persuaded him to invest? A broken engagement makes you seem flakier than being a dude who surfs and plays games on your phone all day. Speaking of—"

She turned over her phone. "I need to do my *Phrase Fusion* puzzle while I'm thinking about it. Otherwise, with everything that's going on, I might forget. I don't want to lose my seventy-five-day winning streak. A few months ago, I had a ninety-day streak going. We had to be on set at the crack of dawn and I completely forgot to do the puzzle. So, hold that thought while I do this…"

A few minutes later, she turned her phone over again, victorious after figuring out that day's phrase.

When she looked up at Owen, he had a weird smile on his face.

"What?" she asked.

"Nothing. I didn't realize you played *Phrase Fusion*."

"Oh my gosh, I'm totally obsessed with it. Don't you play?"

He laughed and shook his head. "I'm trying to rehab my image from gamer dude to serious tech mogul. So, nope. I haven't joined the cult."

"Don't judge me," she said. "It's the only game I play now. I gave up all the others, but this one has me totally hooked. I think there's something subliminal worked into the pixels."

"Believe me, I am not judging you. It's just that…
What if I told you…?"

He trailed off, and he was looking at her as if he
wanted to tell her something. She could virtually see
the wheels turning in his head, as if he were weighing
his words.

Ugh. Of course.

He was going to tell her that she was a bad friend. He
was in the middle of a crisis, and she had interrupted
him to play a game.

Way to go, Juliette.

"I'm sorry about that, Owen." She tossed her napkin
over her phone and changed the subject back to where
they'd left off. "I'm just wondering if we go through
with this fake engagement and he agrees to invest in
your project, will there be some kind of penalty when
we break up? Will he pull out of the deal or make you
pay back the money? If that happens, won't you be
worse off than if you just invested that time and energy
into finding someone who believed in you?"

Even though she had a lot more to say, she cut to the
chase. "Thanks for the enticingly romantic offer, my
love, but I think I'll pass."

His face fell.

"I wasn't trying to be romantic," he said.

She grimaced.

"And I was kidding about it being a non-romantic
proposal," she said. "See, that's the problem. Normally,
we would joke about things like this—well, maybe not
things like *this*, because in what universe would we ever
pretend to be engaged? But we've always been able to

joke about everything else. We've barely even broached this subject and already, things feel weird."

He nodded. "I know. It's weird all the way around, no matter how we look at it. If it helps, you're the only person in the world I could even talk to about something like this."

"Oh, I see. I'm the only woman in the world who has ever enticed you to fake propose. That's touching, Owen."

Yanking his chain about this might've been fun if only he hadn't looked so crestfallen.

"Okay," she said. "Let's think this through. Let's say we went through with this. What's the endgame, Owen?"

"I don't know about the endgame," he said. "I don't even have a fiancée—fake or otherwise. Why does there always have to be an endgame?"

"Well, in this case, we kind of need one." Juliette fidgeted, shifting on the hard plastic chair from one uncomfortable position to another. "Unless you actually want to get married."

Stunned that she'd said the quiet part out loud, she clamped her mouth shut, but then quickly added, "Of course, I'm joking. You're my best friend. I don't want to ruin things between us, Owen. Would this ruin things?"

"Not unless we let it, and I won't let it." He picked up his coffee and took a long pull, then set it down and looked her square in the eyes. "Remember after the graduation party, when we promised if we weren't married when we were thirty that we'd marry each other?"

Electricity zinged through her body. He remembered that?

"Yeah, I remember that," she said. "You remember that?"

He nodded.

"You were so drunk, I had to drive you home," she said. "But you must not have been that bad off if you remember those details."

"If I remember," he said, "I guess I wasn't *that* drunk."

She still dreamed about the way he'd kissed her as if it were yesterday.

It was the one and only time they'd kissed.

The one and only time they'd crossed that line from friends to…something more.

If he hadn't been *that* drunk, what did that mean for the kiss, and why hadn't he mentioned it? She'd always chalked it up to him not being himself, not knowing what he was doing. However, the feelings it stirred up in her had been the most real thing she'd ever felt at that point in her life.

Should she mention the kiss now?

But first, she needed to know what he had meant when he'd said he hadn't been *that drunk*.

What did it mean for the thirty-thirty proposal he'd made—that if they hadn't met their matches by this time in life, they'd come back to each other?

Because here they were, both single and in their thirties, talking engagement. Albeit a fake engagement.

She hated herself for wanting to think that this fake

engagement might turn into something real. And that he'd really meant it when he'd issued the thirty-thirty offer and then kissed her.

Suddenly shy, she couldn't form the words. Instead, she trained her gaze on her barely touched bagel, afraid he'd see straight into her heart. Even after all these years, he was still good at knowing when she wasn't saying exactly what she was thinking.

Now, she wasn't even sure what she was thinking.

"Look, I appreciate the position you're in," she finally said. "I'm afraid if we pretend to be engaged, people will get hurt."

Namely, me.

"As it is right now, when I go home, I can break up with my anonymous fiancé with little collateral damage. No one has met him. No one, except for my mother, has any expectations or vested interests."

"Your mother thinks you're engaged to me."

"My mother was on drugs when she said that. After she comes out of the procedure and her confusion goes away, she probably won't even remember any of it. If she does, I'll remind her we are friends, and my actual fake *fiancé* can fade away, and she can call me a spinster and consider it another one of my screwups."

He snorted. "A spinster? That's funny. It's not like you're an old woman. And as far as screwups go, you probably have the least number of screwups of anyone I know. Well, except for my brother Forest, but he's… he's Forest. Real estate mogul, youngest mayor of Tinsley Cove. Now he's married."

"That's right," Juliette said. "Him and Avery Anderson getting married was unexpected. Almost as shocking as the two of them eloping to Paris. In fact, my mom was just saying that out of all the people in town, she thought Forest would've had the most lavish and traditional wedding."

"At least that's one bar I don't have to try and reach," Owen said.

When they were growing up, Owen had confided in her that it had been difficult to live in his older brother's shadow. She'd always told Owen he made his own sunshine. He wasn't Forest and no one expected him to be. The only reason he'd ever live in Forest's shadow was if he put himself there.

"As I've always said, nobody expects you to live up to Forest's standards."

"Well, it's not a bad benchmark to strive for—"

"Except he's not you. You're not him, Owen. Why do I get the feeling that there's more to this proposal than you're telling me?"

He'd been looking down, tearing at the edge of his bagel wrapper.

"How do you know there's something?"

"Because I know you, and I've just got a feeling. Come on, out with it."

"Maybe this is a good reason why we should get married for real."

Her heart thudded.

He's kidding.

He. Is. Kidding.

"You have this uncanny way of knowing what's going on," he continued. "It's like you have a special kind of radar. But you're right that I have a reason. I just turned thirty-one and I don't have much to show for myself."

He looked at his hands as if weighing his words. Finally, he sighed. "This is a lot to ask. I understand if you don't want to do it. It's one thing for your mother to misunderstand your situation, but it's a completely different thing to ask you to join in a charade like this."

He raised his head and looked her in the eyes again. "You're off the hook. No hard feelings, okay?"

Off the hook? Wait a minute.

A nanosecond after he'd canceled the fake engagement proposition, her stomach flipped and she was full of regret for saying no.

All of a sudden, everything snapped into place and she knew what she had to do.

"I'll do it," she said.

"You'll—you will?" He looked stunned.

"What's wrong?" she asked. "Don't tell me you already have liar's remorse?"

"No. I just realized it was a lot to ask and—you don't have to, Jules. I don't want you to feel pressured."

She smiled. "Look, I said I'd do it. You'd better take me up on it while I'm saying yes."

She smiled and raised an eyebrow to let him know she was only partially kidding.

"But I do have to say, that wasn't exactly the proposal I've always dreamed of."

A wicked look flashed in his eyes, and the next thing Juliette knew, Owen was out of his chair and had dropped down onto one knee next to her.

"Juliette Kingsbury—Jules, my best friend, will you make me the happiest man alive and be my fake fiancé?"

"You know I will."

Of course she would. She'd never been able to say no to Owen McFadden.

Not then. Not now.

Owen scanned the oceanfront deck that ran the length of Natasha Allen's parents' house to see if Jules had arrived at the wedding weekend kickoff cocktail party.

It was still early.

Yesterday, Helen Kingsbury had made it through her medical procedure without complications, and she had been released into Jules's care that afternoon. One of Helen's friends, Ginny, had volunteered to stay with Helen tonight so that Jules could attend the party.

Jules's mom still lived next door to the Allens. He'd offered to stop by and pick Jules up so that they could walk to the party together, but she'd declined.

For a good reason.

As soon as the medication that had relaxed Helen for the procedure had worn off, she hadn't said another word about Jules and him being engaged.

With that, he and Jules had decided to keep their *betrothal* on the down-low until after the wedding so as not to cause a stir and upstage Tasha and Jack's weekend. The news was bound to surprise a lot of people, and they had agreed that since they weren't really engaged, it wouldn't be right to take the spotlight off their friends. Besides, he hadn't had a chance to break the news to his parents.

He and Jules had discussed what their arrangement would entail. Best-case scenario was that Richter would congratulate him and invest. The more complicated case would be him wanting to meet Jules.

So, whether or not to let Bert and Bunny in on the ruse hinged on Richter's reaction. Even then, they'd agreed that the fewer people who knew, the less messy it would be.

His parents would be surprised.

They'd always liked Jules, but his mom was friends with Helen, who usually kept Bunny filled in on who Jules was dating. In fact, a few months ago, his mom had even mentioned that it sounded like Jules was serious with Ed.

He couldn't remember what he'd said. Only that he'd been relieved when his mom had later lamented that Helen had said Jules and Ed had broken up.

Was it wrong of him to be relieved that the relationship had fallen through? He wanted Jules to be happy, but frankly, the guy had sounded like a self-important jerk. The dude was some kind of a director or producer…something notable in the film industry.

In all fairness, Owen hadn't met the guy, but from the things Jules had said and the way he seemed to dangle jobs in front of her like a carrot, Owen had concluded that she was better off without him.

Owen glanced in the direction of the Kingsburys' house, but he didn't see any sign of Jules. When he looked away, his gaze snared with Kimmy Ogilvie's. Her face lit up and she sauntered toward him, arms outstretched.

"Owen McFadden, you gorgeous man, come here and give me a kiss this instant," Kimmy demanded.

Owen didn't even have to move, because Kimmy closed the gap between them. Getting into his personal space, she tipped her face up to him expectantly. Obligingly, he dipped his head to kiss her on the cheek, but she turned her head at the last minute, put one hand on either side of his cheeks and kissed him soundly on the mouth. It wasn't a deep-throated kiss, but it lasted a moment longer than a friendly kiss hello should have.

That was vintage Kimmy. She might've changed her look, but her MO was still the same. She was still the same go-after-what-she-wanted kind of woman. That could not be disguised. He'd known from the day they'd broken up that she wasn't the one. She'd been fun. They'd had a great time while it lasted, but that had been the end of the road for them.

"Kimmy, how have you been?" he asked after he'd extracted himself from her.

"Just fine, Owen," she said. "But after seeing you, I'm much better now."

She lifted her left hand to smooth her hair, and her diamond ring caught the light.

"What's this?" He took her hand and looked at it.

"What does it look like?" she asked coyly.

"It looks like a rock on your left ring finger," he said. "Are you engaged?"

"I am!" she cried. "Are you jealous?"

Owen laughed. "Why would I be jealous? I'm happy for you. If you're happy, I'm happy."

She nodded. "But *shhhhh*! Don't tell anyone else.

This party is for Jack and Tasha. I don't want to steal their thunder on their wedding weekend. Still, I think this calls for a toast, don't you? Be a darling and go get us some champagne."

She hadn't changed a bit. She was still issuing orders and he was doing her bidding. Only this was different. They hadn't spoken in thirteen years, and to be honest, he'd only thought of her in passing, and that was when something had come up that jogged a memory.

As he approached the bar, Kimmy's laugh transcended the party chatter and music. Owen glanced back and saw her talking to a couple of guys who had been his friends back in the day. Jack still kept in touch with them, but Owen had lost track of them over the years.

Kimmy still loved being the center of attention. The way she was flashing around that rock on her finger, her engagement wouldn't be a secret for long.

When the bartender approached, Owen asked for a flute of champagne and a scotch on the rocks.

When he turned to take Kimmy her drink, he saw Jules step through the French doors that led from the Allens' living room out onto the deck. The wind blew her long blond hair into her face, and after she'd brushed it out of her eyes, she saw Owen and her smile was brighter than the full moon hanging over the ocean. Owen smiled back and mouthed, *I'll be right there*.

Jules met him over at the group where Kimmy was holding court. Owen handed Kimmy her champagne flute and then hugged Jules, taking care not to spill his drink on her.

"How's your mom doing?" he asked.

"She's okay. Her friend Ginny was a little late, and then I had to give her the rundown of what Mom could do and shouldn't do. I think Ginny understood, but I'm not so sure about Mom. She's dead set on doing everything herself. I had to resort to telling her that if she was fine, which she isn't, she didn't need me to stay here for the next month. That got her attention, but the truth is that she really does need to take it easy for a while until her body heals."

As Owen nodded, he felt someone's gaze on him. He looked over and saw Kimmy watching them.

"Juliette," she said. "It's so good to see you again. Did you tell Owen your big news?"

Juliette frowned. "I just got here, and I thought we had agreed—"

"Oh, *pffffft*." Kimmy waved her bejeweled hand as if clearing Juliette's objection from the air. "Nonsense. Tell him. Or I will."

Jules glared at her.

"What's your big news?" Owen asked, playing along.

"She's engaged, too." Again, Kimmy's voice transcended the music, conversation and the roar of the ocean waves. "Our little Juliette is getting married, Owen."

Owen put his arm around Juliette and pulled her close.

"I know," he said. "I'm the lucky guy."

Kimmy blinked rapidly and forced a fake smile that looked as awkward as a slapdash application of lipstick. Her gaze pinged back and forth between Juliette and Owen, and soon enough, her bewilderment narrowed into a conspiratorial smirk. As if she'd finally figured out that Jules was the butt of a colossal joke.

Until Owen took Juliette's hand.

"It's true," he exclaimed. "We're getting married!"

Everyone turned and looked at them.

"Oh, no," Jules whispered under her breath. Owen gave her arm a reassuring squeeze.

"But wait a minute." Kimmy crossed her arms and raised her chin. "How could you two be engaged? You live on opposite sides of the country from each other."

"There's such a thing as a telephone and FaceTime," Juliette said.

Kimmy shook her head as if it didn't make sense. "You haven't even given her a ring, Owen. I mean, really?"

"I was saving that for when we were together," Owen said. "You know. A proper proposal."

Jack and Natasha swiftly approached them, arms linked. "Down on one knee, son," Jack said. "Let's see it."

"No, not now. I, *uh*… I don't have the ring with me. Plus, I want the moment to be perfect."

"Good guy," said Natasha. "You only get one chance for the perfect proposal. But I have a question."

She narrowed her eyes at Jules. "Why is this the first I'm hearing of this?"

Juliette's eyes grew large. "Oh, you know…this week belongs to you and Jack. I wanted all the attention to be on the two of you. Isn't that right, Kimmy? In fact, Kimmy and I were discussing that the other day when we ran into each other at the bridal salon."

Kimmy offered a one-shoulder shrug. At least she had the good grace to look embarrassed.

She raised both shoulders and said, "Everyone knows I've never been any good at keeping a secret. How often are we all together like this? I figured we should celebrate together."

"That is a fantastic point," said Natasha. "I'd rather share the happiness than hoard it."

Someone nearby pinged a champagne glass and hollered, "Give her a kiss!"

A rousing cheer went up, and people Owen knew, and others he'd never seen before in his life, chanted, "KISS! KISS! KISS! KISS!"

He grinned at Jules. She looked so small standing there, and it made him feel fiercely protective.

She stared back at him wide-eyed and unreadable. Her cheeks were flushed a pretty shade of pink. He tried to gauge her thoughts on the matter—should they seal the deal with a public kiss? It certainly would make everything more…real. They hadn't talked about the logistics of their agreement. Clearly, they needed to do that…the sooner the better.

He did know Jules well enough to understand that she hated being the center of attention. They hadn't thought this through. All he'd known was that after she'd confessed that her engagement wasn't real, he'd felt as if he'd been granted a second chance. Then when Dan Richter had questioned his seriousness, the fake engagement seemed like the perfect solution for both of them. He wasn't sure he wanted to marry anybody, but he knew damn well that he didn't want to lose Jules to someone like Ed, who didn't deserve her.

He needed to do the right thing and diffuse this situation. He was just about to tell the crowd that, while they appreciated the congratulations, this evening belonged to Tasha and Jack—when Jules licked her lips, leaned in and kissed Owen soundly on the mouth.

Her lips were soft and lush. Yet the kiss was surprisingly direct and commanding.

As if his body had a mind of its own, his arms went around her waist, pulling her closer.

As she sank into him, he breathed in her clean, floral scent and was transported back to that time long ago on the front porch…the one and only time they'd kissed… The truth was, he hadn't been as drunk as she'd thought he was. He'd had just enough liquid courage to loosen him up so he could kiss her goodbye.

He'd had so much to say about how he really felt about her, but somehow all that came out was some asinine verbal spew about them marrying each other if they both were still single when they were thirty.

The next day, when he had gone to see her, to tell her what he'd really wanted to say, she was gone.

They'd gotten into different schools. She'd gone her way and he'd gone his.

Even though they'd kept in touch, they'd never talked about that night. He'd written a letter to her, telling her how he felt, but he'd never sent it.

And here they were again. More than a dozen years later, some crazy circumstances had brought them full circle. Only, this time, he was stone-cold sober, and she was tilting her head so they could deepen the kiss that was supposed to just be for show.

The kiss sent waves of electricity pulsing through every fiber of his body. Desire pooled low in his belly. His body was alive in a way he hadn't experienced in years. In fact, he couldn't remember the last time he'd felt this way.

As his arms tightened around her, he knew he was putty in her hands.

Finally, the sound of applause broke through his haze-clouded brain.

When they broke apart, he searched her bewildered-looking eyes, cupped her face and kissed her one more time, before they joined hands and turned back toward their audience.

At the very least, they were both a couple of damn good actors, because clearly, they had convinced the crowd they were the real deal.

"Since we're announcing our good news, I should let you know that I'm engaged, too." Kimmy held up her bedazzled hand in authentic spotlight-back-on-me fashion. "Don't forget about me. I still can't believe this gorgeous ring is mine."

For the first time in her life, Juliette was happy for all the attention to be on Kimmy Ogilvie.

Juliette needed time to process that kiss.

Pheeew. That kiss.

She watched Owen approach the bar, and that warm feeling she always got when she looked at him blossomed in her chest. It was a feeling that had always lived inside her and surfaced every time she thought of him. The feeling had matured over the years. It was no longer the heart-pounding, stomach-scooping, roller-coaster-ride reaction that she used to have when she'd been in middle school...and then in high school. Nor was it how she'd felt during the first years of college, when they'd arrange to meet for spring break, or the years they'd both been broke and had to opt for stay-cations at their parents' houses and hung out together.

As the years had gone on, that feeling had become less fireworks, more sanctuary—she'd known Owen was someone she could trust with her heart and soul.

Probably because they'd never ruined things with sex.

As Juliette watched Owen walk toward her with their flutes of champagne, she had a fleeting thought that if he'd ever seemed remotely interested in her sexually, she would've chanced it.

And no doubt she would've lost everything, which seemed to be her favorite party trick.

Thank goodness the universe had protected her from herself.

He handed her one of the flutes, clinked glasses with her and then leaned in and whispered, "We need to talk ASAP."

Her heart sank. "Okay. After the party?"

He shook his head. "Let's go for a walk on the beach."

So, he wasn't kidding when he's said ASAP. Well, she wasn't going to apologize for taking the lead and kissing him—if that was the problem.

Good grief.

All of her defenses went up. He'd certainly pretended to be a willing participant. If she'd offended him then… then… Well, they'd need to set some ground rules so they'd be better prepared if they found themselves in a similar situation again.

Owen tried to hold her hand as they made their way through the crowd, but she had a champagne glass in one hand and pretended to need the free hand to hold up the hem of her gold-and-white maxi dress as they navigated the steps leading from the Allens' deck down to Tinsley Cove beach. The sun was setting, and a warm breeze was blowing, cutting through the humidity. They walked until they were far enough down the beach that they could no longer hear the party sounds.

"I barely said hello to Tasha," she said. "We shouldn't be away too long."

"She and Jack will have us all weekend," Owen said. "I think they can spare us for a few minutes."

Juliette laughed. "They probably won't even know we're gone."

"You're probably right. Feel like sitting?" Owen motioned to a patch of soft sand in front of the dunes.

They sat with their knees touching. It was so natural, this contact.

"So, the word is out now," she said.

"Yep."

"You didn't have to tell everyone we were engaged."

"Since Kimmy had backed you into a corner, I was concerned that you might blurt out Ed's name. My stepping up was preemptive."

She wondered if he was jealous. He sounded like

he was, but he was probably just protecting his story for the investor.

"You never liked Ed, did you?" she said. "Even though you never met him."

Owen snared her gaze. "Are you upset?"

Juliette took a deep breath and blew it out in a steady, measured stream.

"No." She drew squiggles in the sand with her finger. "You know how news travels in Tinsley Cove. Now we need to tell our parents, unless we want them to hear about it secondhand.

"Have you already told Dan Richter that you're—that *we're* engaged? If not, Owen, maybe you shouldn't—"

"Too late to turn back now." He put his hand on her arm. His touch unleashed a kaleidoscope of butterflies that swarmed and dipped in her stomach. "A good portion of Tinsley Cove just watched us announce our engagement."

And kiss.

Her lips still tingled. She bit her bottom lip to make it stop, but she could still feel his mouth moving on hers as if the kiss had been real.

Well, technically, it *had* been real.

She wished it had been real in the emotional sense, too. A realization washed over her. She needed to guard her heart because she was in danger of falling hard and getting hurt.

"We need to do something to help us keep things in perspective," she said.

"We do?"

"Yes—I think we should set up some ground rules."

He looked confused. Of course he did, because he wasn't in danger of getting hurt.

"Are you upset because I kissed you?" he asked.

On the contrary, dude. That's why it's dangerous. To you, it's a means to an end. To me, it's quicksand, and I'm already in up to my chin.

"We need something to keep us grounded," she said, sidestepping his question. "Think of it as our rules of engagement."

"I suppose rule number one would be to not kiss you again," he said. "I'll try, but people like to see people in love kiss."

"It's kind of creepy if you put it that way," she said. "But no, I know tonight couldn't be helped. And for the record, *I* kissed you."

He smiled. "Yes, you did."

She rolled her eyes, then shrugged. "We'd be kidding ourselves to think that we might not find ourselves in that situation again."

"So, you're saying kissing is *not* off-limits?" he asked.

"Let's cross that bridge if we come to it...again," she said. "For now, to keep ourselves grounded and not get carried away with this charade, let's share one true thing with each other every day."

"Every day?" he asked.

She nodded. "Well, every day that we see each other."

"Which will probably be pretty much every day," he said. "Don't you think? If we're going to keep up this... charade."

"Probably," she said. "If we want to be convincing.

People who are engaged enjoy spending time with each other."

"Then what's today's one true thing?" he asked. "You go first. Show me how it's done."

She blinked. "Oh, okay. Since I just came up with this rule… I'm not really prepared."

"Just tell me something that's true," he urged.

She racked her brain and spat out the first thing that came to mind—before she could change her mind. "You do know that this isn't the first time we've kissed."

"Yep," he said.

When he didn't elaborate or qualify the first kiss, she continued. "You were pretty drunk. I just wanted to make sure you remembered."

"We already established that I wasn't *that* drunk that night after the party."

She nodded. "Yeah, we talked about what you said that night, not what you—what we did."

"We kissed." He smiled at her, and she was relieved that he seemed so comfortable talking about it. "Tonight's kiss was every bit as good as I remember that first kiss being. That's my truth and I'm sticking to it. On that note, we'd better get back to the party."

He stood up and offered her a hand, which she accepted. He pulled her to a standing position. As they made their way back to the Allens' house, she replayed the conversation in her head, trying to make sense of it.

He'd been so casual talking about that first kiss. Not that he needed to make a big emotional deal out of it.

Her own private truth—her own number one rule of

engagement—needed to be that she understood that their first kiss had meant more to her than it meant to him.

Otherwise, he would've brought it up over the years. Wouldn't he have?

Chapter Four

"You don't have to walk me home, Owen," Jules said. "I'm only going next door."

"Is this where you're staying?" Owen joked. "What a coincidence. I used to know a girl who lived here. If I remember correctly, she was pretty cool."

They'd left the party as soon as people had started to move toward the door. Jules had said she didn't want to leave Helen with her friend too long.

Still, Owen wasn't quite ready to say good-night to her. Not yet.

"Oh, yeah?" she said, pausing at the bottom of the front porch steps and turning toward him. "I heard she was super cool."

"Yeah," he said. "I hear she still is."

She laughed and rolled her eyes.

He shoved his hands into his front pockets as he battled the urge to lean in and kiss her again. If he shifted forward just a few inches and closed the distance between them…

Something had shifted after that kiss on the deck. Something between the two of them—or maybe it was just him. Maybe it was the way she'd brought up the original kiss from all those years ago. They'd never talked about it before tonight.

He wasn't sure why.

He'd wanted to talk to her about it. In fact, the next morning he'd gone to her house, but she'd already left. He'd written her a letter spilling his guts, but he'd never sent it, talking himself out of it because she'd left without saying goodbye.

In reality, she had said goodbye. She'd driven him home. He'd kissed her and she'd left. That was a pretty firm goodbye.

Now, here they were.

She was the one who had initiated the kiss, and then she'd brought up that night.

Here he was, wanting to put it to the test again, wanting to push the envelope.

"Wild night," he murmured, kicking at a stray pebble on the walk with the toe of his shoe and watching it as it rolled into the mulched flower bed.

"Are you okay?" she asked.

When he looked up, she was smiling at him, but her brows were knit, giving away her uncertainty.

"Me?" he asked. "Yeah. Are you okay?"

"If you've changed your mind about the engagement—"

"I haven't changed my mind. Why would you think that?"

"Because you're acting weird. What's going on?"

I want to kiss you again.

What would she do if he was just honest and told

her the truth? He wanted to kiss her again because that kiss earlier had done something to him.

He pulled himself to his full height and gave her his best smile.

"I'm fine. I'm good."

"Okay, then."

"Are you free tomorrow?" he asked. "We should probably break the happy news to our families. That is, if your mom is up to it."

Jules nodded. "I think we should. Let me see how she's feeling, and I'll touch base in the morning. Tasha is treating the bridesmaids to brunch tomorrow. So, maybe we can do it earlyish?"

Owen nodded. "Sure. I'm sure I can make it work. I'll text my parents and tell them I need to talk to them."

She took a deep breath, let it out and smiled. "I guess we're really doing this."

"Yeah, we are," he said, following her up the porch steps, stopping in front of the door. "I'll see you tomorrow."

He opened his arms, and she leaned into the hug as if it was the most natural thing in the world. Especially when she tilted her head up and looked at him. For a moment, time stood still. Then a force greater than him had him lowering his head so that his mouth could meet hers.

As their lips brushed, the front door opened.

"Juliette?" asked Helen. "Oh, it's you and Owen. Hello, there."

Jules jumped away as if something had burned her.

"Mom, what are you doing?" Juliette asked. Her cheeks were flushed. "Shouldn't you be lying down?"

"Nonsense. I feel perfectly fine." Helen smoothed her gray, chin-length hair into place. "In fact, I feel better than ever. The doctor was right. That pacemaker is making all the difference in the world. I just can't raise my arms over my head, but that will come soon enough."

"Helen? What are you doing?" Another voice sounded from behind Mrs. Kingsbury.

"I'm talking to my daughter and her fiancé, Ginny," Helen said, an edgy note coloring her voice.

Jules and Owen shared a look, but Owen still caught the sheepish expression on Ginny's face. "I just stepped away for a moment to use the little girl's room. I had no idea she'd answer the door while I was gone. Helen, please go sit down and rest."

"Now, Ginny, you know good and well that I am not an invalid," Helen said. "The least you could do is congratulate the kids on their engagement."

"You're engaged?" Ginny grabbed Jules's hand, looking for a ring. "Oh! Well, that's fine. Congratulations! I had no idea you two were even dating."

You and the rest of Tinsley Cove.

"In fact, come in," Helen insisted and motioned them inside.

As they stepped into the foyer, Ginny continued congratulating them.

It was interesting that Helen still believed they were engaged even though she hadn't said anything more about it after her surgery. Obviously, she was still under the impression that they were getting married. All the better for them. That was one less person they needed to tell before word got out.

Mentally, he crossed her off the list of people he and Jules would have to inform—unless someone from the party had already called her. If that was the case, then maybe someone had told his parents, too?

If so, he would explain that Kimmy Ogilvie had run into Jules at Primrose Bridal and had announced the news prematurely at the party. It wouldn't be ideal, but his parents were reasonable. They'd understand. They'd cut his older brother Forest some slack after he'd eloped with his girlfriend, Avery.

Since Avery had no immediate family, Bunny McFadden had looked forward to pulling out all the stops on her oldest son's wedding, but plans had changed when they'd returned from Paris married. Bunny had been disappointed, but she'd welcomed Avery to the family with open arms and treated her like her own daughter.

"I know you two just came from a cocktail party," Helen said. "But I've had a bottle of bubbly in the refrigerator for ages just waiting for the right occasion. I couldn't think of anything I'd rather celebrate than two of my favorite people getting married."

He and Jules exchanged a fleeting glance, and he knew they were wondering the same thing. Why had Helen fixated on Owen being the one? Rather than rousing suspicion by asking questions, he decided to go with it.

"Juliette, will you be a dear and help Ginny pour the

champagne? You'll have to use wine glasses. I'm sorry I don't have those fancy-schmancy champagne glasses that are proper, but I hope you'll see that the sentiment is still heartfelt."

Helen smiled and gave a one-shoulder shrug.

He had a feeling that she might have been embarrassed that she didn't have the finery that his parents had now, but after all those years that they'd been next-door neighbors, before his parents' real estate business had taken off, Helen should know that his parents were grounded and had brought up their kids to be the same way.

"Helen, it's nice of you to open the champagne for us." He slipped an arm around Jules's waist and felt her stiffen. "As far as I'm concerned, we could drink it out of paper cups and I would appreciate it just as much as if it had been served in fine crystal."

Helen tittered. "You are such a good man, Owen McFadden."

The moment Jules disappeared into the kitchen, Helen said, "I noticed Juliette is not wearing an engagement ring. Do you have plans for a ring?"

"We were just talking about that earlier," he said. "I wanted to make sure I got her something she liked."

Helen jumped to her feet and clapped her hands. "I don't mean to be a buttinsky, but I would be honored if you would give her my granny's engagement ring. My granny wore it. My mother wore it. I wore it. It would be just wonderful if my Juliette would carry on the tradition. When she was little, if I took it off to wash my hands or do dishes, she would put it on and admire it. I always promised her someday it would be hers."

"It's nice of you to offer, Helen," Owen said.

She cast an assessing look in the direction of the kitchen.

"Wait here. I'll be right back."

As Helen headed down the hallway, Owen took out his phone, noted the time and dashed off a text to his dad asking if he had time to see him tomorrow morning. If his parents had heard the news, surely he would have received a phone call by now. It was getting too late for people to be making congratulatory calls tonight, so most likely they were safe until the morning.

Seconds after he sent the text, the dancing bubbles that indicated Bert was typing appeared on Owen's phone screen, and a message came through saying he and the rest of the family had an early meeting with Dalton Hart, the executive producer of *Selling Sandcastle*, but Owen was welcome to drop by the Sandcastle Real Estate office anytime.

He thought about mentioning that Juliette might be with him, but instead opted for a quick, See you in the morning, before Helen returned with a small black velvet box, which she presented to him on her extended palm. "Open it."

He opened the hinged lid, and a modest round diamond winked at him from the box as if it were in on the conspiracy. The stone was nestled in an old-fashioned square white-gold setting—or it might have been platinum. He wasn't sure, and it seemed rude to ask. The square setting was encrusted with additional tiny diamonds. It was delicate and feminine and—

"It's perfect for Jules," he murmured.

"I took off my wedding and engagement rings two years to the day after my Vincent passed," Helen said. "I figured that way I wouldn't lose them and I could save them for Juliette when the special day arrived. It was lucky for the previous three generations. It brought us happy marriages." She clasped her hands under her chin and beamed at Owen. Then her smile grew tight. "I just wish my Vincent could've lived to see this day." She nodded resolutely. "Even so, I'm so happy you want to use the ring. Maybe you can use the money you would've spent on a ring for a down payment on a house. Now, I do have to say, I have some money in savings for the wedding. It won't be anything grand, but I'll do the best I can to give you and Juliette the best wedding celebration I can. But with that ring—I know you've already proposed, but I was hoping you might do it again and make it special when you give her the ring. Will you do that for me?"

Owen found himself nodding through the overwhelming feelings that were settling on him. All this talk of diamond rings and house down payments and wedding ceremonies. He'd have to make sure Jules stopped her before she spent a penny on anything wedding related.

Helen seemed so happy.

He hadn't counted on feeling this way. As if he were lying to a woman who had been like a second mother to him.

Actually, *they* were lying to her.

It was a lot for a simple charade, and it made the reality of it feel very heavy. Because it was also part of the plan that they would break up in the not-so-distant future. He hated the thought that Helen would be the one who got hurt in the end.

Jules had mentioned it before they'd agreed to go through with the ruse, but it hadn't sunk in.

Jules and Ginny came back into the room, each carrying two half-full wine glasses. Unsure of what to do, Owen closed the ring box and stuffed it into his pocket. Before he made a big deal out of the ring, he wanted to talk to Jules and make sure it was what she wanted.

Obviously, it was the best of both worlds. He had a ring to give her. A ring she wouldn't have to pretend to give back to him after she broke off the engagement.

They clinked glasses and sipped and made small talk. Helen and Ginny took turns peppering them with questions, such as whether they'd given any thought to setting a date or which wedding venues they preferred, because all the good ones were reserved far in advance, and if they wanted their first choice they shouldn't wait. The two older women insisted they should put down a deposit as soon as possible.

He let Jules field those questions since this was her mother.

Owen was glad he'd switched to seltzer and lime after that initial scotch and a sip of the champagne toast. He knew he'd be driving. So it had seemed like the responsible thing to do. Plus, he wasn't the party animal that he used to be. Generally, he got up early, and when he did stay up late, he was usually working and needed a clear head.

He didn't have the tolerance or taste for alcohol that he used to, but he played along.

"Owen, what did your folks say when you shared the good news?" Ginny asked.

He cleared his throat. "We, uh, haven't had a chance to tell them the happy news yet."

Helen's mouth fell open. "Oh, for heaven's sake. Why not? Why haven't you told them?"

Owen took Jules's hand and laced his fingers through hers. She squeezed a little too hard and glanced at him as if saying, *This question is all yours. I handled the others.*

"Oh, well, you know... Jules just got back into town. Helen, you've been under the weather, and we've been busy with Natasha and Jack's wedding."

"But it did come up tonight at the cocktail party," Jules said. "Kimmy Ogilvie was delighted to share that she ran into me in Primrose Bridal wearing a wedding dress."

"Oh, dear," Helen said.

"You kids need to tell them as soon as possible," Ginny said. "I am happy to stay with Helen whenever you need me."

Helen scoffed. "I don't need a babysitter, Ginny."

"I know you don't," Ginny said. "But I'm dying to watch the rest of season four of *Downton Abbey*. I have to know what happens with little Marigold. I don't get the show through my streaming service."

Helen shrugged. "Well, in that case, why not?"

"I'm meeting my family at the office in the morning around eight," Owen said. "Does that work for you all?"

Ginny nodded.

Jules said, "I need to be at La Marais by eleven o'clock for the brunch that Tasha and Mrs. Allen are throwing for the bridesmaids, but other than that, I'm free."

After the plan was in place for tomorrow morning, Jules walked Owen out onto the front porch.

With the front door firmly closed between them and Helen and Ginny, Jules sighed and said, "That was so weird."

"I know. I kept thinking that your mom was going to announce that she'd seen right through everything I was saying and knew this was all a ruse. She has this uncanny way of making me feel like I'm fifteen years old again and she's caught you and me sneaking out to go to a kegger on the beach."

Jules laughed. "Remember when that happened? I thought I'd be grounded for the rest of my life."

They laughed at the memory as they watched the last of the guests trickle out of the Allens' house and get into the few remaining cars that were parked along the road.

They'd almost kissed again, but Helen had interrupted them.

He still wanted to kiss her, but Jules's body language warned that it wasn't a good idea. Her arms were crossed and she was keeping a respectable distance between them.

"Why do you think your mom has latched on to this—" He gestured back and forth between the two of them, not quite sure what to call it. A ruse? An engagement of convenience? Helen seemed convinced that it was real.

Jules shrugged. "I don't know. I didn't name any names when I told her I had someone special in my life. For that matter, I never said I was engaged. She jumped to that conclusion all on her own. At first, I was chalking it up to her not feeling well, not being herself because of the heart condition, and then being all drugged up before she went in for the pacemaker procedure. But she's acting more like herself since she's been home… other than believing we're engaged. I guess she's always hoped you and I would end up together."

His pulse quickened at the thought.

And there it was again.

That indefinable…something.

Was that how people who had committed in real life felt after they'd taken the leap? But he reminded himself that even if the feeling felt real—and was sizzling and flaring between them like a live wire—this wasn't a real life commitment.

Owen reminded himself that if he lost sight of that one true thing and tried to reach out and embrace it for anything other than what it was, they both might get burned in the worst possible way.

There was no turning back. This ship had already sailed. He just hoped that, when it was all over, their friendship was still as strong as it had been going into this crazy endeavor.

"One true thing," he said and ran his hand over his jacket pocket, feeling the shape of the ring box.

"Do tell," Jules said.

"While you and Ginny were pouring the champagne, your mother gave me this."

He pulled the ring out and opened the box.

Jules gasped. "Grandma Willa's ring."

She tore her gaze from it and searched his eyes.

"She wanted me to propose to you with it."

She tilted her head to the side. "You were supposed to have already proposed."

"I know. She wanted me to do it again."

"Okay. Go for it."

"Okay, um… Juliette Margaret Kingsbury, will you marry me?" His voice shook. Then, after realizing that it sounded like he was actually proposing to her, his hands holding the ring box started shaking. He cleared his throat. "Er—I should've said, will you *pretend* to marry me? Or, I guess what I mean is, will you pretend to be engaged to me? And make me the happiest man in the tech business."

Okay, that was bad.

His thoughts were confirmed by the look on Jules's pretty face. She looked as if she had smelled something rotten.

"Is that the best you can do?" she said. "Because, if so, I'm afraid it's a solid no from me."

He frowned at her, then shrugged.

Then it was as if she'd read his mind, as she'd done so many times over the course of their friendship.

"First of all, when you propose—or even fake propose—you should get down on one knee. Come on,

Owen, you should know better than that. You did it in the hospital cafeteria."

"I've never done this with a ring," he said.

"Clearly."

She smiled, and her left brow shot up in the way it always did when she seized an opportunity to tease him.

She gestured toward the ground. "Come on. Down you go."

Before he could second-guess himself, he dropped to one knee.

"Now, take my hand." She held it out, and he did as she'd asked. "Now, try again."

He dropped on one knee in front of her. "Juliette Margaret Kingsbury, will you *pretend* to be engaged to me?"

"Of course I will."

He took the ring from the box and slid it onto her finger.

They both stared at the ring on her finger as it glittered under the porch light. He felt like he should say something or kiss her.

Instead, Owen cleared his throat. "I guess I'll pick you up at seven thirty in the morning, and we'll break the news to my parents."

"You make it sound as if we are about to tell them that we're getting a divorce rather than getting married. Remember, we don't have to do this if you don't want to." She twisted the ring he had just put on her finger like a fidget spinner. As if she had caught herself, she stopped and crossed her arms. "If you want me to, I can go back in there and tell my mom that we came to our senses and called it all off."

He crossed his arms, mirroring her stance—or maybe he was protecting himself from the strange ache that gripped his chest at the thought of doing just that.

The truth was, he needed her more than she needed him. That had been clear since the day all those years ago that he'd finally realized he had real feelings for her.

He'd written everything out in a letter to her, but before he had been able to give it to her, she'd left to make her way in this big, wild world.

He could've sent it. He probably should've sent it, but he didn't because he figured all the near misses were the universe's way of telling him they were never meant to be more than good friends.

Even now, she was his best friend. She was helping him out. But somehow pretending to be engaged to her made it feel as if it could happen.

"Tomorrow morning, let's share our *wonderful news* with Bunny and Bert."

Owen had offered to pick Juliette up, but she'd politely declined since she was going to the bridesmaid brunch, and who knew how long this little errand would take.

As she steered her mom's Honda into the parking lot of Sandcastle Real Estate, she was strangely jittery. She probably shouldn't think of her jitters as strange. They were justified. After they told Bunny and Bert, there would be no turning back.

That would be it.

This was the last chance to turn back and do the right thing—not to lie. Otherwise, it was all aboard the farce express. Do not pass Go, do not collect two hundred dollars.

And now she was mixing her metaphors.

Sort of.

Her hands were on the steering wheel, and the soft morning light glinted off her family's ring—the ring that stood for real commitment...for happy marriages that her parents and grandparents had worked hard to achieve until death parted them. The ring was chiding her for making a mockery out of the holy sacrament of marriage.

"I can't do this," she said aloud. "He will just have to understand. He'll be able to find another means to finance his business venture."

She was just about to start the car and leave, but Owen pulled in beside her and flashed that smile that still melted her heart and made her do things she knew she shouldn't be doing—such as pretending to be engaged to him.

Because, one day, he would meet the woman who swept him off his feet and made him want to commit for real and it wouldn't be her.

Or maybe Owen would never get married.

Maybe he would choose to remain single—

He rapped on her car window. She motioned for him to walk around and get into the car on the passenger's side. He did.

His brown hair was still wet from the shower, and his square jaw had sprouted a shadowy stubble of a beard.

And darn it he smelled good.

She wanted to lean over and bury her face in his neck

and pretend as if the world didn't exist. As if that didn't prove how out of her mind she was right now, she knew she was going to do this even though every fiber in her body was screaming that it was a dumb idea.

But she'd realized that they were the only ones who knew about the deception. When they eventually broke up, they would simply say that they'd changed their minds and had agreed to remain good friends.

It didn't have to be so difficult. She just needed to stop overthinking it, and she needed to make sure they were on the same page.

"You okay?" he asked.

"I'm fine," she said. "Are you?"

There was that smile again.

"I couldn't be better," he said. "Today, I am telling my parents that I'm marrying my best friend."

She stared at him blankly.

"Only you're not really," she said. "Don't get carried away there, bucky."

"I'm just getting into character."

She rolled her eyes.

"You look pretty," he said.

She'd chosen a pink sundress. Actually, it was what she'd planned to wear to the brunch, so it wasn't as if she'd dressed for him… even if she had been thinking about him.

She couldn't stop thinking about him.

"Thanks," she said. "Owen, I know you said you don't like dealing in end games, but we need a plan. I've been thinking about our exit strategy. Once you have the financial backing you needed and my mom is well enough for me to return to Los Angeles, we should quickly and quietly call off the engagement. Okay?"

He blinked, and she couldn't read his expression.

"Okay." His voice was flat.

Her stomach twisted and knotted. Why did this feel like a real breakup? Because it wasn't and feelings like these blurred emotions so early in the game were the reason they needed to know how this would end.

It would be a touchstone to keep them grounded in reality.

That's what she desperately needed, because right now, she wasn't sure if he looked disappointed or if she was just projecting.

"Okay then," she said. "If anyone asks about the breakup, we say my life is in LA and yours is in Tinsley Cove. We decided we were better off remaining close friends."

She bit her bottom lip and waited for him to respond. Instead, he reached up and swept a stray blond curl off her cheek, and the tender gesture made goose bumps sprout on her arms.

She hoped he didn't notice and crossed her arms.

"What time are your parents expecting us?"

"We didn't set a specific time. Dad just said that he had an early meeting and I could come anytime."

"Did you tell him I was coming with you?" she asked.

He shook his head. "It was all done through text as your mother was in the other room getting the engagement ring. There wasn't a lot of time to get into detail. If I would've told him you were coming with me, he would've asked why, and that would've opened a can of worms I really didn't want to get into last night."

She nodded. "I see your point."

"Shall we?" he asked.

As he started to open the car door, Juliette put a hand on his arm. "Owen, wait. We know how this ends, but how did this happen? I mean, we need to get our story straight before we go in there. I probably should've led with this, but don't you think this is going to come as a surprise to them? We didn't have to justify it to my mom because she's not quite herself these days and she loves you. She probably feels like she willed us to be, because this—" she gestured back and forth between the two of them "—this is something she's wanted for decades."

His expression softened, and he was smiling at her as if this were real. The way he was looking at her... It was dangerous. No. It couldn't be dangerous if it wasn't real.

"If it will make you feel better to come up with a narrative, sure. We can do that."

She tried to speak, but the words caught in her throat.

Owen reached out and took her hand. "Jules, you're shaking. It's going to be okay."

He pulled her into his arms, and she got her earlier wish about burying her face in his neck. She took a deep breath and decided right then and there that she could live the rest of her life right there in the sanctuary of his arms, breathing him in and closing out everything that wasn't them.

She wasn't sure how long they had stayed like that,

but the sound of someone rapping on the driver's side window startled her back to the real world.

It was Owen's mother, Bunny. She was bending down so she could see inside the window as she held a brown Bankers Box, which was balanced precariously on her left hip. She was waving at them with her free hand.

Juliette felt a bloom of heat burning deep in the area of her décolletage and creeping its way up her neck to her face.

Oh, good grief. Juliette felt like a teenager who'd been caught making out in a car.

Owen seemed as stunned as she felt. He was sitting there staring at his mother through the closed window. Finally, Bunny made a motion of cranking open a window the old-fashioned way.

When the window was down, Bunny smiled at them and arched a perfectly shaped brow. She looked victorious, as if she'd solved a riddle that had stumped everyone and was damn proud of herself for doing it.

"Good morning, you two. Owen, I don't imagine that this has anything to do with what you wanted to talk to your father and me about, does it?"

Chapter Five

After Owen and Jules delivered the news of their engagement to the McFadden family, Bunny clapped her hands. "Well, I think this is just the best news I've heard in a long time."

She got up from the table and hugged Jules.

Bert extended his hand to Owen. "Yes, indeed, this is wonderful."

As the rest of the McFadden family sprang to their feet, showering the couple with hugs and congratulations, Dalton's voice transcended the celebration. "Are you pregnant?"

What the hell?

The room fell silent, as if Hart's rude question had been a gust of wind that had blown out a candle.

"You have to admit it's kind of unexpected," the reality TV producer said.

White fury clouded Owen's peripheral vision, as every person seated at the conference room table—his parents, his siblings and sisters-in-law and his cousin—turned and gaped at Dalton, but only for a moment. Then they turned and looked at Jules and Owen, waiting for the answer.

Owen had gone against his gut feeling that warned that it would be a bad idea to break the news to his parents while Hart was in the room, but his entire family had gathered in the conference room along with Dalton and a few members of the *Selling Sandcastle* crew. They were having an early production meeting to nail down next week's shooting schedule.

The timing hadn't been ideal. Owen would've preferred telling his family privately, but after last night's kiss, it was only a matter of time before word got around. He and Jules had obligations for Tasha and Jack's wedding today. Basically, it had boiled down to now or never.

Another irrational surge of anger reared up inside Owen. He could feel it contorting his face and causing him to ball up his fists under the table. Jules must've sensed his rage, because she reached out and covered one of his hands with hers, giving him a reassuring squeeze.

"Nope," she said. "I'm not pregnant. We've just decided to get married. To each other."

After a beat of stunned silence, Bunny clapped her hands again. "Well, as I said earlier, I think this is wonderful news. Lucy, honey, go get a bottle of champagne out of the refrigerator in the kitchen. This calls for a toast."

With that, the McFadden family resumed their celebration.

Through the chorus of good wishes, Owen heard Dalton say, "Well, I'll be damned." He leaned back in his chair and crossed his arms over his chest. "I never would've put you two together. Not in a million years."

Dalton had been a few years ahead of them in high school, and he hadn't traveled in the same circles as Owen and Jules—during or after school.

"Weren't you with that Kimmy—what was her last name?" Dalton said. "The hot blonde."

Again, Jules squeezed his hand under the table. Only this time, he wasn't sure if it was a signal for him to keep calm or because she was tempted to deck the guy herself.

"Dalton, bless your heart," Bunny said and beamed at the couple. "I am not one bit surprised. They've been good friends since they were little kids, and frankly, friendship is the best foundation on which to build a marriage. I am simply delighted by the news. But Dalton, honey, if I may be blunt, even if they were expecting, that's nobody's business but their own. We are not living in the dark ages."

She slanted him a look that packed more of a punch than if she had continued the verbal upbraiding.

Dalton had the decency to look sheepish.

Good, thought Owen. *As he should.*

The guy had no filter. In fact, Dalton had never had one. Not for as long as Owen had known him. That character flaw, the ability to shamelessly ask the rude questions without flinching—questions that everyone in the room was probably wondering, but had been too polite to ask—was what made him good at producing reality television.

That's why Owen had wanted out of the reality show

Selling Sandcastle after he'd gotten his taste of the conflict that Dalton wanted them to manufacture. Owen had been part of the show during the first three seasons, but he had recently distanced himself from it, walking away from the fame and the money it brought him, because he hated the way the show had painted him as an irresponsible ladies' man who floated through life, mooching off his parents.

Even though they'd grown up in the same town, Dalton Hart had no idea that Owen was the mastermind behind *Phrase Fusion*.

Now all he had to do was leverage the success he'd achieved from the game to launch SmartScape Technologies. It would be the sustainable win he so desperately needed. Then he could tell his family about *Phrase Fusion*, and what others had viewed as creative dalliances would be vindicated. Rather than seeing him as a dilettante or a dreamer, they'd look at him with respect.

He'd almost told Jules about *Phrase Fusion* when they'd been sitting in the hospital cafeteria, but he knew she'd ask what was next. Since the subsequent games he'd developed had been a bust and the smart home tech venture was hanging on by a thread, even though she was his best friend—the one person in the world he could confide in and be real with—he was at the point in his life where he wanted something to show for himself, for his efforts, so that she didn't see him as the surfer who played games all day.

Thanks for reinforcing that image, Hart.

Dalton Hart loved to find a person's Achilles' heel and bring them down—on national television.

In the show's first season, Dalton had heartlessly outed his sister-in-law Cassie's most personal secret on national television, almost causing his brother Logan to break up with her. In season two, Dalton's target had been Owen's older brother, Forest, and his girlfriend, Avery. In the third season, he'd humiliated Owen.

He should've seen it coming, but he'd been completely blindsided. He was lucky Hart hadn't done some digging and found out Owen was behind RomeO Enterprises and *Phrase Fusion*.

That's why Owen had bowed out of this final season.

He didn't get a charge out of hurting people or fighting with them or prodding and poking them where it hurt the most just to watch them squirm, which had to be the reason he was feeling ultraprotective of Jules right now.

He wondered if his parents had broken the news to Dalton that the show had run its course.

Selling Sandcastle had actually been his mother's brainchild. Barbara "Bunny" Bradshaw McFadden had come up with the idea of a reality show that followed the day-to-day workings of their family business, Sandcastle Real Estate. She had been the driving force behind getting their longtime family friend, Dalton Hart, to produce it. Bunny had called in favors from her contacts in the Junior League and the chamber of commerce. She'd hired the best photographers to showcase the family's agency and the town of Tinsley Cove in its best light, all of which helped Dalton realize that his former hometown was a picture-perfect location for a reality show.

It had all paid off when everything had come together and Dalton had agreed to do the show. Then, two weeks after receiving the good news, disaster had struck: Bunny had been diagnosed with breast cancer.

Her family had rallied around her and promised her that when she got well, they would all do their best to make the show happen. Even their younger brother, Logan, had uprooted his life to move back to Tinsley Cove from California. Bunny's treatment plan had worked and she remained cancer-free.

Healthy and happy, she'd had the time of her life during the show's first three seasons—especially because her four kids were all living close by. Nothing meant more to her than being surrounded by her big, boisterous family. However, Owen knew his mother well enough to suspect that the shine of starring in a reality show had worn off, as had living in the constant presence of television cameras.

It just wasn't a sustainable lifestyle for a family like theirs.

After Lucy had returned with the champagne and everyone had toasted Jules and Owen and settled into their chairs around the table, Dalton said, "Did you get all of that, George?"

For a moment, Owen wasn't clear who George was or what Dalton had meant when he'd asked if the guy had gotten *all that*.

All what?

It became crystal clear the minute the stocky guy who had been sitting in the back of the conference room stood up, revealing the small camera he was holding.

"Got it," George said.

"What exactly are you talking about?" asked Owen.

"You and Juliette announcing your engagement to your family," Dalton said, as unaffected as if he'd just given his lunch order. "The champagne toast was a nice touch. Great idea, Bunny."

Owen and Jules exchanged an alarmed look. She shook her head, her eyes huge.

Even though Owen had a good idea of what Dalton planned to do with the video recording he'd shot so stealthily, he decided to give him the benefit of the doubt, which was more than the opportunist deserved. "What exactly do you plan on doing with the footage?" Owen asked.

Dalton smiled and answered, in a condescending, singsong voice, "We'll be using it in the show, of course."

Owen felt as if the wind had been knocked out of him, but somehow, he found his breath.

"No," Owen said. "You will not be using it."

"Yes, I will." Dalton smiled as if this were a battle of wills and he intended to be the last man standing.

"You can't use it if we refuse to give our permission," Owen said. "I didn't sign a contract for this season because of what you pulled last time, Hart. Jules has never been a cast member, and I won't let you drag her through the mud."

"Not a problem." Dalton waved off the issue as if he were delivering good news. "We can remedy that with a simple release. We just need a quick signature. We will even pay you. Standard rate for a featured extra."

When both he and Jules shook their heads, Dalton said, "Come on, you two. Owen. Dude. You owe it to your fans. They need closure."

Owen laughed. "Fans? I don't have fans."

"Yes, you do," said Dalton. "And people get attached. Since this is the last season—your folks just broke the news to me today—you need to let them know you're okay. It breaks my heart that your folks don't want to continue, because we have a good thing going here. But because we're ending the show, we need to show all of you sailing off into the sunset, living your best lives. What better way to do that for you than for your fans to see you happily engaged—or better yet, depending on when the wedding is, we could work it into the show. It would make a fabulous finale."

Dalton held up his hands, thumbs together, making a three-sided frame.

"I can see it now," he said. "The show can follow you and Juliette as you plan the wedding. All the ups and downs that go into a life-altering event such as this."

He stared at the space between his hands as if he could see the scene unfolding in the middle distance.

"It's going to be great," he murmured. "As an incentive, I'm fairly certain that I could find some money in the budget to help defray the cost of your nuptials. That is, if you allow us to film the big day. And as many scenes as we'll need leading up to the wedding, of course."

Owen snorted. Clearly, this guy didn't understand the meaning of the word *no*. Somehow, from a clear refusal about using the footage of them announcing their engagement, he'd gotten a storyline that included a finale wedding.

"Thank you, but no," Jules said. "This is a private matter. It's between Owen and me…and our families. I'm not comfortable with any of it being aired on national television."

"Why not, Juliette?" asked Owen's cousin Lucy. "You work in movies. I mean, like, real movies. In Hollywood."

Owen glared at her. "Lucy, you're not helping here."

Lucy put her hand over her mouth and grimaced as she murmured an apology.

Ignoring Owen's objection, Dalton stood and faced Jules, holding his arms open wide. "Well, there ya go. You're a natural, Juliette. We'd love to have you on the show. You know, with all this material, we might as well make both of you full cast members. It's going to be great."

Obviously shaken, Jules shook her head and shot Owen a pleading look.

"Yeah, that's not going to happen," said Owen as he pushed away from the table and stood. "You might as well get that through your head right now, Hart. We need to go."

As he and Jules walked toward the conference room door, Hart called after them, "A beach wedding would be nice. Very photogenic, with the blue sky and water in the background. I'll let y'all think about it."

They paused in the reception area, then Jules exhaled a breath in a whoosh and rolled her eyes. "That was brutal."

Before she could say anything else, Bunny came around the corner.

"Juliette, hon, I'm sorry about that. Sometimes Dalton gets ahead of himself. I'll talk to him and ask him to stand down. In the meantime, Owen, sweetheart, take this box with you."

She gestured to the Bankers Box she'd carried inside earlier and had set on the front desk before going into the conference room. "I should've just had you put it in the trunk when we were in the parking lot, but, well, you know. We were all a little distracted, if you know what I mean." She blushed. "I knew right then and there something romantic was afoot."

She waggled her eyebrows as if they all shared a secret.

"What is that?" Owen asked, redirecting their attention to the box.

"It's just some mementos from your old room at the house," she said.

"Okay," Owen said. "That's not too bad if it all fits into one box. I thought there would be a lot more."

Bunny shook her head. "Oh, honey, that little box is like a bucket of water out of the ocean. When your father told me you'd be here today, I figured I'd at least get you started. I took that box directly from your closet. But I'll need you to come over and go through the rest of your things. There are yearbooks and surfboards and all kinds of other sporting equipment that I couldn't even begin to name."

Before he could tell her just to donate it all, she had pulled Jules into a hug.

"Lovie, I can't let you leave here until I tell you how excited I am that you and Owen have finally decided to take this step. I didn't want to say anything in front of Dalton after you made it clear that you want to keep this private—and I don't blame you one bit. Dalton is just being a little pigheaded right now because we'd just broken the news that this would be our last season." She shook her head. "That's just Dalton being Dalton. He'll get over himself soon enough. But just between us, I must confess, I didn't even realize you two were dating. How did all this happen? What kind of a mother am I if I had no idea what my middle son was up to?"

Owen nodded in the direction of the conference room. "That's probably something we should talk about when we're sure one of Dalton's men isn't going to pop out of the woodwork with a camera."

Bunny gasped. "You are absolutely right. In fact, this is a discussion that demands a nice dinner and a bottle of wine. Juliette, as soon as your mother is feeling up to it, after Tasha and Jack's wedding, I want to have the two of you over for dinner. How does that sound? Then you and this son of mine who tells me nothing—" she ruffled his hair in mock frustration "—can give me all the details."

"That sounds wonderful," Jules said.

"Good," Bunny said. "I'll be in touch."

After they said their goodbyes and he and Jules had let themselves out of the office, the reality of what they'd just bitten off settled in.

Dalton had latched on to that narrative like a bulldog

locking on to a leg of lamb. That meant it was imperative that they get every detail of their story straight.

People like Dalton had an uncanny talent for sniffing out irregularities—especially if it was fodder for one of his shows.

For all they knew, he might already have caught on to their charade.

If that was the case, he would be looking for any chance to expose them, whether or not they chose to be on *Selling Sandcastle*.

The following Saturday, surrounded by friends and loved ones, Tasha and Jack exchanged wedding vows, promising to love each other until death tore them asunder.

As Juliette stood at the altar, with the five other bridesmaids clad in identical pearl-pink mermaid-style floor-length dresses, she had no doubt that the couple would honor this promise.

Tasha was a beautiful bride in her ivory beaded and appliqued tulle princess gown. Juliette was flooded with emotions as she watched her childhood friend marry the man she loved.

Juliette was delighted for the couple, of course. They'd been together for a long time—since high school, as a matter of fact. They had weathered some dire storms along the way, but in the end, they'd always found their way back to each other. If ever there was a testament to true love, it was Tasha and Jack's relationship.

Even so, if Juliette was being perfectly honest, she couldn't help but wonder when it would be her turn.

She would never begrudge her friends the happiness they so richly deserved. Never in a million years. But as she stood at the altar during the ceremony paired with the man *she'd* been in love with for as far back as she could remember, all she could think about was, when would she finally meet the man who would return her feelings and break the spell that Owen had cast on her?

Despite everything, she still believed that somewhere out there was a man who wouldn't only want to pretend to be engaged. When she met him, he would make her fall so deeply in love that she would be able to step back and embrace her friendship with Owen for what it was—a friendship.

Now, at the reception, she sat at a table with her mother and Bunny. Owen's mom—her fake future mother-in-law—had summoned her, saying, "Come sit by me." The two had proceeded to unload all their ideas about wedding venues, potential caterers and flowers that would look just lovely at various times of the year.

Since Juliette couldn't get a word in, all she could do was sit there and wonder how the heck things had already gotten so far out of control. It was starting to resemble the chaos theory, the butterfly effect, in which a seemingly simple and localized happening—such as a butterfly flapping its wings, or two people telling a little white lie—can set in motion events that culminate in huge disasters elsewhere. In their case, the disaster was the inevitability that their mothers would be heartbroken when she and Owen "broke up."

But the butterfly had already flapped its wings big time and things were changing by the minute.

The evening after she and Owen had told his family about their engagement and had been through the mill with Dalton, they'd agreed that it would be best to keep their story simple.

The official line went like this: they'd kept in touch over the years via telephone and video calls and finally realized that they were more than friends, that they belonged together. Actually, it was the truth—well, minus the love epiphany—they *had* kept in touch. They talked at least once a week—usually more—even when she was on location. A couple of times, when Owen had been away on business and had been close to Los Angeles or the location where she'd been shooting, he'd stayed with her.

Once, about five years ago, when Owen had been working as an IT manager for GreenHarbor Initiative, which was a sustainability project aiming to create eco-friendly solutions and promote environmental consciousness within communities, he'd won a trip for two to Eleuthera in a raffle at the company Christmas party. He'd invited her to join him. She had happened to be between projects, so she did.

As the mothers chatted, Juliette scanned the room and found Owen standing at the bar talking to a couple of the groomsmen. He laughed at something one of them said, and his gaze snared hers. He raised his brows in that flirty way of his and flashed that smile that never ceased to rearrange her insides.

Did he ever think about their Eleuthera trip?

They'd had as much fun as two best friends could

have. Sleeping on separate double beds in the one bed-room, they'd given each other adequate privacy.

It was on that trip that Juliette had pondered the *what ifs*… What if they just…tried each other on for size? Just once…because they'd shared everything else over the years.

You know, sort of a what-happens-in-Eleuthera-stays-in-Eleuthera kind of vacation between friends.

But she hadn't been able to find the words to bring it up, much less say, "I want to make love to you. Let's do it just this one time and we never have to speak of it again."

Had he ever even had a fleeting thought like that about her?

Oh, how she wished he had.

But in Eleuthera, Owen had been the perfect gentle-man, giving her plenty of personal space. He'd sworn off alcohol during that trip, too. Who quits drinking right before they go to the Bahamas, where the rum is cheaper than the orange juice? So they hadn't even had the opportunity to blame it on a night of rum-fueled bad judgment.

Maybe he'd stopped drinking because he didn't want to put himself in the position of having a drunken roll with his best friend. If she had a dollar for every hour she'd lain awake dissecting the particulars of that trip… Well, she wouldn't be a wealthy woman, but at least she'd have a healthy nest egg.

With a wink of one of his sea-glass-green eyes, he turned his attention back to the guys.

She laughed to herself. Had he really just winked at

her? That was the flirting equivalent of a dad joke, and she fully intended to razz him about it later.

She'd ask him, *If you were trying to pick up some hot babe in a bar, would you wink at her?* She already knew that he'd say, *Hell no, I save all the special looks like that just for you.*

So, yeah, coming full circle, their story was rooted in reality.

If anyone thought the two of them falling in love was implausible, it would be their problem. Because even Dalton would be hard-pressed to find a smoking gun that he could grab and brandish as proof positive that their engagement was a farce.

Not if they kept it simple and stuck to the script

"I need all the single ladies in the middle of the dance floor," the DJ announced. "Calling all the single ladies." He played a snippet from the Beyoncé song before fading the music and saying, "We have a bouquet to toss. If you're engaged, that means we want to see you, too."

"Come on, Juliette." Kimmy seemed to appear at the table from out of nowhere. "We may be engaged, but we haven't pulled the trigger yet. That means, technically, we're still single."

"I don't know if I agree with that," said Bunny. "If you are engaged, you are not a single lady, but bouquet tosses are fun, and if this is what the bride wants, then who are we to disagree? Y'all get yourselves out there on the dance floor."

"Hello, Mrs. McFadden," Kimmy gushed as she put her diamond bedazzled hand on Bunny's arm, not bothering to greet Helen. She pulled a grimace-smile and drew her shoulders up to her ears. "I was so excited for Juliette and Owen when I heard the news. Not gonna lie, though. I was super surprised to hear it. I mean, Juliette Kingsbury and Owen McFadden? Who would've ever thought those two would end up together?"

Bunny reached in front of Kimmy and took Juliette's hand. "If ever two kids were meant for each other, it's these two. Growing up, she spent plenty of time at our house. In fact, Bert and I consider her a second daughter. We could not be happier."

Bunny beamed at Juliette as if she really meant it. And she did, because she wouldn't have said anything if she didn't.

Juliette's stomach knotted up with a longing so profound that it made her want to curl up in fetal position and lose herself in the misery of what she couldn't have. Instead, she had to dig down deep and muster the smile of a woman who was betrothed to the love of her life.

Juliette supposed that most people carried around their own secret sadness, that everyone had their own crosses to bear. She'd carried hers for such a long time that sometimes she even forgot that she shouldered it. Until something would remind her of Owen—something she remembered him saying, or something happened that she knew would make him laugh, or just something that she wanted to tell him before she told anyone else. Those things threw her off balance and reminded her that she was in love with Owen McFadden. She had been for as far back as she could remember. But he would only ever see her as his best friend.

"Kimmy, when are we going to meet your intended?" Helen asked.

"Oh, everyone calls me Kimberly now." She flashed a perfect smile. "And as for Richard, well, you know, he's busy, busy, busy. Such is the life of a thoracic surgeon. He's in such demand that we almost never get out of Atlanta these days, but…"

She fidgeted with her engagement ring, turning it around on her slim finger before shrugging. This time, her smile seemed forced and there was something in the set of her jaw that gave Juliette pause.

Hmm… Maybe everything isn't as perfect in paradise as Kimmy—er—Kimberly wants us to believe.

"But you must be thrilled that Owen is still in Tinsley Cove," Kimberly said. "And I hear he's turned out to be quite the entrepreneur."

Back in the day, when Kimmy had dated Owen, and on those awkward occasions when a group of them had been hanging out together, Kimmy would talk to everyone but Juliette—as if she were trying to render her invisible or at least pretend like she wasn't there—and it used to get to Juliette.

But it didn't anymore.

Now, it just seemed desperate.

After all these years, this woman still needed to be the center of attention. She still needed to ice people out to build herself up.

"As I said, I am so happy that Owen is finally settling down and Juliette and Helen will be part of our family," Bunny said. "There was a day when I feared Peter Pan syndrome was going to cost Owen his business—he is my late bloomer. He's the last of my boys to get married. I'm glad he took his time, lived life a little before he settled down. As a single man with no one to support but himself, he could take chances on this business idea he's launched. Bert and I are real proud of him. You know, we offered to give him a loan for his business, but he politely refused. He said he had to do things his own way, in his own time. I'm proud of him for that, and I have no doubt he will be successful."

It was clear that Bunny was saying this for Helen's benefit so that she would know that her daughter would be in good hands. But Kimmy was drinking it all in like a dog lapping up spilled gravy.

"It's wonderful that you believe in your son, but Juliette, we're going to miss the bouquet toss if we don't get out there."

As she and Kimmy walked silently to the dance floor, Juliette could hear Bunny and Helen making plans for a family dinner sometime that week.

By the time they were in place for the bouquet toss, they were at the back of the bunch.

After Tasha turned around and made eye contact with Juliette and smiled, Kimmy took a few steps forward, positioning herself in front of Juliette. Tasha tossed the flowers in a fast-traveling, high arch that carried the bundle up and over the pack, perfectly in line with Juliette.

Even though Kimmy reached for the flowers like a wide receiver trying to catch a pass, the bouquet landed right in Juliette's arms. In the aftermath, Kimmy got her hands on the flowers, and it looked like she was about to grab them from Juliette. Maybe she had a moment of self-awareness, or, more likely, the horrified expressions of the other women standing around them had registered. She pulled both of her hands away, lifting them like a cop had told her to put her hands in the air, and said, "Oh, okay. I'll let you have it."

"I thought, for a minute there, you were going to challenge me to a tug-of-war," Juliette said.

Kimmy threw her head back and laughed as if it were all a big joke. "No. I have my man."

She held up her hand and showed off her diamond.

Here they were, two grown women, and Juliette had a feeling this continued rivalry wasn't about who caught the flowers as much as it was still about who was receiving Owen's attention.

Even though Kimberly was sporting the Rock of Gibraltar and had landed herself a surgeon, clearly, she still couldn't stand to see Juliette with Owen, who just happened to catch the garter.

When the DJ invited Juliette and Owen to join Tasha and Jack on the dance floor for a special spotlight dance to the Ed Sheeran song "Thinking Out Loud," Kimberly was nowhere to be found. Or at least Juliette didn't see her among the wedding guests crowded around the dance floor and seated at various tables watching the couples dance.

Yes, she'd looked. Because she'd wanted Kimmy to see her dancing with Owen, but Kimmy's whereabouts seemed less important when Owen wrapped his arms around her waist and pulled her close. Juliette draped her arms around his neck and gazed up into his green eyes.

Being this close to him turned her insides to jelly. She was glad she was holding on to him because she felt a little unsteady on her feet.

Giving her head a mental shake to ground herself back in reality, she said, "Your girlfriend is jealous."

"My girlfriend?" he said, leaning in until his head touched hers. "You're my one and only, remember?"

The *for now* was implied, and it brought her crashing back down to earth faster than anything.

He stepped back and twirled her under his arm at the part of the song that talked about two people finding love right where they were. It was kind of perfect, and it took her breath away for a moment.

If only it were real.

When the music faded, Jack and Tasha were standing by the head table. Jack picked up his champagne glass and tinged it with a butter knife.

"If you will indulge me, I would like to propose a toast to my beautiful wife. Tasha, in every glance we share, every inside joke that lights up your face and every tender touch that speaks volumes, I see the foundation of a union built on the strongest bond of all— friendship. Genuine care and understanding for each other sets our love for each other apart.

"Let's raise our glasses in celebration of love and friendship, two of life's greatest treasures. Because when you marry your best friend, not only are two souls uniting in love, but also two best friends are embarking on a lifelong journey together. And here's to

Juliette and Owen. Two more best friends who finally came to their senses. You're next, guys."

As she swallowed the ball of emotion that had lodged itself in her throat, she could only hope she would be left standing after her arrangement with Owen was over.

Chapter Six

Seated around his parents' dining room table with his folks, Jules and her mother, Owen watched Helen dab the corners of her mouth with the white cloth napkin that had been in her lap.

"Carol Allen stopped by the house yesterday," Helen said. "She and Natasha would very much like to throw an engagement party for the kids after Tasha and Jack return from their honeymoon. She said it's the least they could do after all Owen and Juliette did to make Natasha and Jack's big day so special. I thought it was awfully sweet of her to offer."

Helen scraped the remnants of the crème brûlée Bunny had made to cap off their special family dinner, which had started with a hearty coq au vin.

"That's just wonderful of her." Bunny sipped coffee from the delicate Wedgwood Florentine Turquoise china cup. The only reason Owen knew the name of the china was because his mother had driven home the fact that her Wedgwood china was special because it had been her wedding china. That's why they only used the dishes for special occasions. Bunny would wash every piece by hand. Growing up, special occasions had been the rare instances when the McFadden siblings were excused from washing the dishes, because Bunny had always said, "If anyone breaks a piece of my Wedgwood Florentine china, I want it to be me."

Tonight, she was focused on something else entirely. "Aren't Jack and Tasha home in a few days?" Bunny asked.

"I believe so," Helen said.

"Do you suppose Carol and Tasha would have time to get together with us next week?" Bunny nodded to Juliette to signal her inclusion in the word *us*. "We could compare calendars and set a date for the party. I don't suppose you two have given any thought to a wedding date?"

Owen slanted a glance at Juliette. She'd plastered a smile to her face, but judging by her silence, he sensed that underneath she was silently freaking out.

He took her hand and gave it a reassuring squeeze. *I've got you. Don't worry.*

"That's great," he said. "It was nice of them to offer to throw a party for us. You know me, any excuse for a party."

"It is nice of them," Juliette said, suddenly snapping to. "Since Tasha and Jack's wedding was just last week, we haven't had a moment to think about dates."

"Well, now, as I said, you don't want to put it off too long," Helen said. "Otherwise, all the good churches and reception venues will be taken. I thought since you two have been talking all this time that you might've tossed around some dates."

Juliette made a *hmm* sound.

"Nope," Owen said. "Not yet."

"I'm grateful that Carol Allen would want to do this for us," Juliette said. "But throwing a party is a lot of work. I'm sure she's exhausted after all the wedding expenses and hoopla they've been through recently. Now they want to incur the expense of yet another party?"

As if of one mind, Helen and Bunny frowned at Juliette.

"Hoopla?" Helen's voice went up an octave on the "hoop" part of the word. "Why in tarnation would you call it hoopla? A wedding is a celebration of love, honey. An engagement party honors your intent to commit."

"Yes, and it was very gracious of Carol and Natasha to offer," added Bunny.

"I've known Carol Allen long enough to know that she doesn't offer things like that offhandedly," Helen added. "If she extended the offer, she meant it, and you should be grateful."

"I *am* grateful," Juliette said. "I just don't want her to go to a lot of trouble."

Jules shot Owen a pleading look, and he stepped in.

"You know Jules. She's always hated for anyone to make a fuss over her."

"He's right," Jules said. "It makes me uncomfortable. That's all."

A slow smile spread over Bunny's face. "And that's one of the many reasons we love you, dear. You're so humble, but I'll tell you what, darlin'. You're not in La-La Land. You're in the South. So you'd better get used to people making a fuss over you. You're going to be a bride. In Tinsley Cove, weddings are a big deal. Everyone gets sentimental seeing the kids they've watched grow up, fall in love and forge a life together. You're the next generation. Really, it's a rite of passage, and everyone feels some ownership in the days leading up to your nuptials. I wouldn't be one bit surprised if several people offer to throw parties and showers for you—friends of your mama's, friends of mine. Maybe it would help to think of it this way. It's not simply a party for you and Owen. Many will want to do something to honor your family. It's an enviable position to be in to have such a support system—especially since you've been away for so long. Just try and let go and enjoy it, honey. Will you do that?"

Juliette nodded and soon the conversation shifted to other matters.

Even though Juliette had done a good job making the family believe she was amenable to the idea of a season of parties leading up to the big day, Owen could sense that she was unnerved.

After the table was cleared, Owen asked her, "Want to take a walk?"

"I would like nothing more," she said.

Bert had excused himself to the TV room. Bunny was bustling around the kitchen making more coffee for herself and Helen. They seemed to be intent on planning this wedding on their own.

"We'll be back in a bit," he said as he took ahold of Jules's hand. "I need to walk off some of this dinner. Otherwise, I might never eat again."

"You and me both," Juliette said. "Thank you, Mrs. McFadden. Everything was delicious."

Bunny looked up from the French press coffeepot. "No more of this Mrs. McFadden business. You're not a teenager anymore. You're going to be family. Honey, please call me Mom."

An *eerp* sound escaped Juliette's throat. She managed to smile, but Owen watched the color slowly drain from her face.

"We'd better get going before it gets dark," Owen said, covering for her.

They left the house via the French doors that separated the family room from the back porch.

When the doors were shut tight behind them, Juliette said, in an urgent, hoarse whisper, "Your sweet mom asked me to call her Mom."

Owen nodded.

"Owen, I can't call her Mom, because the only reason she asked me to call her that is because she believes we're getting married. And now your mom and my mom are in there planning the wedding, and the Allens want to throw us an engagement party—"

He put his finger to his lips and motioned to the beach.

They walked toward the yard and the neat rows of Italian cypress trees that his father had planted when they'd first moved in. Tonight, they stood tall and proud, like sentinels standing guard along the perimeter of the yard leading down to the beach. The trees were Owen's favorite thing about the house. Bert and Bunny had worked hard to make the home an oasis— inside and out—for their family over the years. The sprawling Italian villa was a far cry from the modest home they'd traded it for, which was next door to the one that Juliette's mother still lived in.

Moving in at age fifteen, Owen had only lived in the larger house for three years. It was no wonder the place had never really felt like home to him. His parents, however, had put so much of themselves into it, and it had been such a point of pride, a symbol of their success, that it was strange to think of his folks selling the place and moving on.

"That's so pretty," Jules said, gesturing to the ornate lighted fountain situated in the center of the back patio. It featured a large lion with water shooting from its mouth into the stuccoed reservoir.

Owen nodded.

It reminded him of something that should be in an Italian piazza. It and its larger counterpart, a fountain in the middle of the circular driveway out front, seemed out of place with the backdrop of the Atlantic Ocean, which rested at the foot of the sprawling backyard. While Owen considered the statues and ornaments a bit over the top, his parents had taken such pride in them.

"Did you know my parents are selling the place?" he asked.

Juliette's eyes went wide. "What? I didn't know. Wow. It's the end of an era."

He nodded. "Yeah, this place has always meant so much to them, it's hard to imagine them selling it."

He shrugged.

"I know you never felt at home here," she said. "I'm guessing you're not attached enough to miss it once they've moved on."

He shrugged again and shook his head. "I won't miss it. It's their place, and they have to do what's right for them. The house next door to you will always be my childhood home."

She was the only person that he'd told that this place had never felt like home. She was the only one who understood. Even then, he'd kept the venting to a minimum. Who wanted to hear him complain about something so banal? Nouveau riche kid problems.

"Your mom always made me feel welcome when I would come over, but to be honest, when we hung out, it felt like being in a museum."

And that was the reason he and Jules had always worked so well. They both shared the same sensibilities.

"I'd be happy with a house on the beach where I could surf in the morning and work from my home office on my own terms," he said.

"Does anyone really need any more than that?" she said.

As they made their way across the lawn toward the beach, he put his arm around her and pulled her close. It wasn't for show. It was for them. It was what they did.

"How are we going to get out of this engagement party?" When they reached the seawall, she stopped walking and looked up at him. "Owen, I don't want our friends to go to the trouble and expense of throwing us a party. And now with your mom asking me to call her Mom. She's going to hate me when we break up."

"She won't hate you. She could never hate you. She might hate me for letting you go…"

He had a sudden impulse to tell her he wanted to

make this real, but she deserved a proposal that was better than that. Not an impulse born of a fake engagement that was starting to spiral out of control.

Still the question remained: why not?

After the initial shock wore off, almost everyone had said they weren't surprised that they were together. So many had said it seemed like destiny.

Why could everyone else see it except for them?

But before he went out on a limb like that, he needed to make sure his convictions were substantial enough to hold the weight of what he'd be doing. It was one thing to be in on this private arrangement between the two of them, but it was another to suggest that they make it real.

If she said no, what would happen next?

"All I know is that we need to come up with a good reason or two to keep pushing off the party." Jules grimaced and released a full-body sigh. "I don't know, Owen, this just keeps getting bigger and bigger. What's going to happen if we trip ourselves up? I know we said we just needed to stick to the script, but I can't help but feel that we're flirting with disaster."

She shook her head.

"It's one thing to tell a white lie to make my mom feel better, and, you know, even then it really wasn't okay. But when people start spending money on us—and we're not really an *us*—I think we need to quit while we're ahead."

When Helen had first mentioned the party, he'd had a selfish moment where he'd thought that would be the perfect opportunity for him to let Dan Richter know he was engaged. . He'd invite Dan and his wife and introduce them to Juliette, but Jules was right. People had already invested too much in them; it wouldn't be right to allow them to start investing money in the form of parties.

But who was to say they couldn't go to Dan Richter and his wife in California?

"If you want to call off everything, I understand," he said. "I just want what's best for you, Jules."

"Can you find another funding source for your business?" she asked. "I don't want to leave you high and dry."

"Don't worry about it. You know me. I'll figure out something, but before we call it quits, will you hear me out?"

She nodded.

"What if we got out of town for a while," Owen suggested. "Dan Richter, the guy who is interested in investing in SmartScape Technologies, lives in Cupertino. What do you say that we take a trip to California? We could fly into San Francisco. I could introduce you to him and take care of business. We could rent a car and drive down to LA. Maybe you could take care of business, too. See if you could get on with another picture."

She looked uneasy.

"Talk to me," he said. "What are you thinking?"

"It's a good idea, but I need to make sure Ginny can stay with Mom. Mom is the reason I'm still here. And—ugh—this is embarrassing to admit, but I'm a little strapped for cash right now. Until I get work on another movie."

"If we do this, I'm footing the bill," he insisted.

She made a disagreeable noise. "Owen, I don't know about that. I wouldn't feel right letting you pay for everything."

"Think about it," he said. "You could use the time to check in with your contacts and see if you could get on with another production."

"But the reason I'm here is because Mom needs my help," she said.

"What if I offered to pay Ginny?" he said.

"No, Owen. I'll figure out something."

He hopped down from the seawall onto the sand and helped her down.

Because of Tinsley Cove's position on the coast, the beaches mostly faced south. During the spring, the sun was positioned to rise and set over the ocean along the shoreline. Tonight, the sunset painted the sky with vibrant hues of red, orange, pink and purple. Despite the turmoil they were experiencing, the fading light painted a tranquil and peaceful picture around them, as the world prepared to transition from day to dusk.

Looking at Jules standing there in that white sundress, the setting sun bathing her in such a gentle light, Owen's heart squeezed. He knew he would do whatever it took to make her happy. Even if it meant sacrificing this opportunity with Dan Richter.

She gazed up at him. "You know, we kind of got off track with the 'one true thing' we were going to do when we first got engaged." She'd put air quotes around the words *got engaged*.

He nodded. "We have, haven't we?"

We've blurred the line between what's true and what isn't. Maybe that's why things have gotten so complicated.

"I'll go first," she said. "My truth is that sometimes I need a minute to think about things before they make sense to me. Now that I've had a chance to digest it, I think a trip to California makes sense. I was going to suggest that you go by yourself. I mean, they can't have an engagement party without the groom-to-be." She laughed. "But if Richter sees us together, and sees that you're nothing like the way Dalton Hart portrayed you, he might reconsider. If Ginny can stay with Mom, I'll go with you—as long as you let me pay you back for everything."

Owen shrugged. If ever there was a time to pick his battles, this was it. They had plenty of time to negotiate who owed what to whom.

"Now you go," she said. "What's your true thing for today?"

The only thing he could think that seemed true to him right now was that he loved her.

He did.

But they were trying to strike a delicate balance. Maybe now wasn't the best time to freak her out with a declaration of love. Instead, he heard himself uttering the one true thing he'd been keeping to himself.

"My true thing is I am the one who created the game *Phrase Fusion.*"

She smacked him on the arm playfully. "Come on, this is serious. Don't joke."

"I'm not joking."

He told her how he'd created it and why he'd kept it a secret.

"Since none of the subsequent games landed as well, I didn't want people to look at me like I was a flash in the pan. Even now, I'm not ready to let anyone else know."

"I think you need to let Richter know," she said. "Owen, that's a game changer. Sorry, no pun intended. I mean it. It will make all the difference in the world, regardless of whether you created other games. Your smart home technology is important."

He held up his hands. "Maybe. Let me think about it."

"The game is so popular now," she said. "I still don't understand how you were able to fly under the radar."

He told her about the LLC RomeO Enterprises.

She wrinkled her nose. "As in Romeo and Juliette? Like, you and me?"

He blinked, unsure of what to say, but she didn't look freaked out. She was smiling as if she loved the idea.

"Yep. Romeo and Juliette. I guess it's always been you and me."

At once, his heart clenched and his cheeks burned. Blurred lines indeed.

Chapter Seven

*R*omeo and *Juliette*?

She could read so many things into that. As she could read many things into Owen's adorable reaction when she'd put two and two together.

Instead, she focused on persuading Owen to tell Dan Richter about the success he'd had with the game. He'd designed the most successful game in the country. That was impressive and would prove that he was serious and focused.

Never mind that he hadn't created a successful follow-up to *Phrase Fusion*. Gaming wasn't his focus. Smart home technology was.

She'd also asked him if he'd told Richter the impetus behind him getting into smart home technology.

He hadn't.

She'd said, "See, this is why you need me and this is why we have to go to California. You have to tell Dan Richter all this. When he sees how passionate you are, he will know the depth of your commitment."

With that, she had talked to her mother, who had called Ginny, who said her schedule was free and she was happy to stay with Helen the week they'd be gone.

All that was left was for Owen and Dan Richter to agree on a meeting date and they could reserve their flights and lodging.

In the meantime, she was trying not to let her mind run away with fantasies about why he'd called his shell company RomeO.

As in Romeo and Juliette...

"Hello? Juliette?" said Kimmy—er—Kimberly. "Are you there?"

Juliette blinked. Tasha and Kimberly's faces came into focus.

The three of them were having lunch at Le Marais. Kimberly had invited them so that they could catch up and hear all about Tasha and Jack's honeymoon.

"Sorry," Juliette said. "I have a million things on my mind."

"Tasha asked you what days worked best for you and Owen," Kimberly said. "For your engagement party. Is something wrong? You seem like you're only half-heartedly here."

Kimberly laughed and slanted a glance at Tasha, who set down the glass of iced tea she'd been sipping.

"Are you okay, Juliette?" Tasha asked. "It does seem like your mind is somewhere else."

"I'm fine. Really." Juliette smiled and then took a long pull from her own tea glass. "I'll have to talk to Owen about dates, especially since we might be going to California soon."

"Planning a pre-wedding romantic getaway?" Tasha said.

Kimberly flinched and stiffened. It was almost imperceptible, but Juliette was sitting directly across from the woman, and something had made her glance just in time to see the shift in demeanor.

"I highly recommend it," Tasha continued. "Jack and I went to a B and B in Vermont last fall before everything with the wedding kicked into high gear. It was the best thing we could've done for ourselves."

Juliette glanced at Kimberly again. There it was— the tight set of her jaw, which caused her cheeks to draw in, making it look as if she were sucking on a lemon.

"Are you okay, Kimberly?" Juliette asked, turning the tables on her.

Kimberly laughed. "Of course. Why wouldn't I be?"

"I don't know," Juliette said. "You seemed upset for a moment."

Juliette knew from experience that she should've ignored her and turned her full attention to Tasha, but the words had slipped out before she could stop them.

With her fork, Kimberly moved a leaf of lettuce to the other side of her plate, before setting down the utensil and folding her hands in her lap.

"If I'm completely honest," she said, "I'm a little sad these days. Richard is working so much that he doesn't have time for these fun getaways that you're talking about. I guess I'm a teensy tad jealous. But only in the best way."

Her practiced smile spread over her face, and she rotated her diamond ring back and forth on her finger. "Of course, all the time he's putting in now will pay off in the end. You know, we're planning a three-month, seven-country honeymoon after the wedding. Even though we don't have time to indulge in these cute little trips y'all are taking right now, I'll have him all to myself for a good long while when it matters."

As Kimberly regaled them with the seven-country honeymoon agenda, it dawned on Juliette that if things went well while they were in California and Owen was able to lock down the financing, they might be able to call off the engagement before they would be pressed to schedule a date for the party.

Juliette was still trying to figure out why Kimberly had inserted herself into helping Tasha and Carol Allen throw Juliette and Owen's engagement party. It felt almost as weird as her lunch invitation.

Even though they shared mutual friends, such as Owen, Tasha and Jack, Kimmy Ogilvie had never liked Juliette. She had never done nice things for Juliette. In fact, in the past, when she'd been nice, it was usually because she wanted something.

So, in addition to deciphering the *why* behind Owen naming his company RomeO, Kimberly's motives were today's secondary puzzle.

She should've never agreed to come today. She would've preferred a one-on-one lunch with Tasha, but they were all grown-ups now. Maybe this was Kimberly's way of extending an olive branch and proving that, now that they were in their thirties, they could all be friends.

Yeah, right. And if Kimmy had changed, maybe Juliette and Owen would end up getting married for real.

It wasn't going to happen, and if she knew what was good for herself, she'd better be on her guard.

Or just tune Kimmy out.

True to form, Kimmy had spent more time talking about herself and her perfect doctor fiancé than Tasha had spent telling them about her honeymoon trip to Paris, which was meant to be the reason for the lunch.

While Kimmy was doing the humble brag thing, Juliette found herself drifting off back to the RomeO enigma and the sound of Owen's voice saying he wanted to take her to California.

She felt Kimberly's gaze on her.

"So, you'll ask Owen for a few dates when you see him tonight," she said. "Give them to Tasha, and she and I will see if we can settle on one that works for everyone, but not the fourteenth or the eighteenth of next month. The twentieth and twenty-ninth of this month are all out for me, too."

After they'd settled that, they spent the next half hour hearing about the engagement party that Kimberly's sorority sisters were planning for her. Tasha and Juliette would be invited, but the party was in Miami. So Kimberly would understand if they couldn't come.

Juliette tried to shift the conversation to Tasha and Jack's trip to Paris, but inevitably, Kimberly would find a way to steer it back to herself.

Which was why it seemed odd when Kimberly had turned to Juliette and said, "I can't believe you actually live in Los Angeles and work in the movies, Juliette. I'm so intrigued. Can you introduce me to Timothée Chalamet?"

"I would if I knew him, but I've never met him."

"Oh. I see." Her tone took a noticeable downturn,

as if that fact alone proved that Juliette might work on movies, but nothing important.

For at least the tenth time, Juliette racked her brain for an excuse to leave, but she'd endured Kimberly's nonsense so long, it was a point of pride to ride it out to the end.

"Your last location shoot was in Venice, wasn't it?" Tasha asked, clearly in a show of support for Jules. "My gosh, the traveling you've done is nearly as exciting as the movies you've worked on."

Tasha's eyes sparkled.

"Yes, travel perks are wonderful, aren't they?" gushed Kimmy, oblivious. "I've been able to travel so many places on the company's dime since I started working for Eloise Laurent Cosmetics. Mostly domestic, but rumor has it they're going to send the executives to London. I can't wait. I've never been. But what about this *Selling Sandcastle* reality show that Owen's part of? How fun that they've been filming it right here. I'm so intrigued. Who would've thought that my ex-boyfriend would be on TV?"

Kimberly laughed, but Juliette's blood began an irrational slow simmer.

My ex-boyfriend.

Her ex-boyfriend?

"Well, you know this is the show's last season," Juliette said. "And Owen chose to opt out."

"That's too bad," Kimberly said. "At least it gave Owen a purpose."

Juliette frowned. "Don't worry about Owen. He definitely has a purpose."

Kimberly lowered her chin and studied Juliette. "Juliette, I wasn't insinuating anything bad. Of course, Owen has a purpose. He has you."

Kimberly's gaze dropped to Juliette's left hand, which was gripping her iced tea glass.

She gasped. "Look at your ring! You didn't have a ring at Tasha's drinks party and now you do. Let me see."

Digging deep to channel her smitten bride-to-be, Juliette complied and held out her left hand.

"*Awww*, it's so cute."

Cute, huh?

Refusing to react to Kimmy's backhanded compliment, Juliette removed her hand. "I love it. It's been in my family for several generations. So, it means a lot to me."

"Oh, it's from *your* family?"

"Isn't it exquisite?" Tasha said. "I think it's so touching that Helen passed on the ring to Juliette. If you and Owen have a daughter, you can continue the tradition."

Juliette ignored the way her ovaries danced at the thought of having Owen's child.

Instead, she considered telling the story of how each bride who had worn it had enjoyed a long, happy marriage. She couldn't decide what stopped her—that she didn't want to share such an intimate family story with Kimmy Ogilvie or…that there would be no wedding for Juliette and Owen because the engagement wasn't real.

"Well, that's nice," Kimmy said. "At least he saved a ton of money since he didn't have to buy you a ring."

Subtext: Owen was a cheapskate.

Kimberly twisted her own ring, then held up her hand and admired it.

"*Kimberly*," Tasha rebuked.

"What?" Kimberly snapped.

"That wasn't very nice," Tasha said.

Kimberly widened her eyes. "What do you mean? How is Owen saving money that not very nice?"

Tasha held up her left hand and displayed her modest diamond ring and plain gold band. "A huge hunk of bling like yours is generally the exception not the rule. Sentiment can be just as important as price."

"I know that, Tasha. I was only trying to make conversation. Why are you trying to make me feel bad about my ring? If you'd prefer, I can put it in my purse."

"Don't be ridiculous," Tasha said. "It just seems like you've been a little edgy since we sat down."

"Excuse me?" Kimberly said. "Edgy? Says she who is trying to throw shade from a glass house."

"Oh, says she who tries to make everything about her," Tasha said. "Okay," Juliette intervened. "When will we finally get to meet Richard?"

Kimberly curled her lip and slanted a glance at Juliette, looking as though she might tell her to shut up, just like she'd done so many times when they were in high school.

"Come on," Juliette said. "Both of you. Let's not do this."

She wanted to say, let's just get through this lunch. We don't have to do it again. But she stopped herself and looked back and forth between Tasha and Kimberly.

Instead, she said, "It's been such a wonderful lunch." What was one more lie? "I'm eager to meet him."

Kimberly sighed. "Who knows? He's so busy at the hospital. But I want to hear how Owen proposed to you. Because as I was just informed, everything isn't about me. If I'm putting everything together correctly, I'm thinking he proposed twice? Before the ring and after?"

Juliette's stomach fell. She and Owen hadn't discussed specifics of the proposal. They'd decided the fewer the details, the better: they'd kept in touch over the years, fell in love and decided to get married.

"Well, yes," Juliette said. "There were two proposals."

Technically, that wasn't a lie. Owen had proposed the scheme that day in the hospital cafeteria and then he'd proposed again after her mom had given him the ring.

Or I guess that's what you'd call it.

More like fake proposed.

He'd said, *Juliette Margaret Kingsbury, will you marry me?* Then he'd quickly amended it to, *Will you* pretend *to be engaged to me?*

Lovely. The words every woman longed to hear.

Kimmy snapped her fingers. "Come on. Girl, we want details."

Juliette shrugged. "It's really not a great story."

"Every marriage proposal is a great story, no matter how simple. For instance, my Richard proposed to me on the London Eye. We were at the very top when he dropped down on one knee and pulled out this baby."

She wiggled the fingers on her left hand.

"Really? I thought you'd never been to London," Juliette said.

Kimberly's eyes flashed, and she covered her mouth with her bejeweled hand. "Did I say London? I must have it on the brain. I meant Las Vegas. You know, London Eye, Vegas Eye. Same Eye, different city."

She laughed.

Juliette knew what she was talking about, but it wasn't called the Vegas Eye. It was called the High Roller. While the London Eye looked over the River Thames and the ancient city's magnificent architecture, the High Roller provided sprawling views of the casinos and the desert. Not much of a similarity, but it was probably an innocent mistake. Even if it wasn't, one liar to another, Juliette knew she had no right to judge.

That's why she was more than ready to move on, but Kimberly seemed intent on doubling down.

"I can't believe you're not excited about your proposal." Even though she was smiling, there was an edge to her voice.

"I am excited," Juliette said. "It's just personal."

"Is that so?" Kimberly tilted her head to the side and raised her brows, like a teacher hearing that the dog ate the homework. "Tasha, Jules's proposal was personal."

Clearly, she was trying to make amends with Tasha, but that wasn't the worst of it —

Jules?

Owen was the only person who call her Jules. Hearing the endearment fall out of Kimberly's mouth made her cringe.

"It's Juliette, Kimberly."

"Touchy," Kimberly muttered and looked around

the restaurant as if she might find someone more interesting.

Tasha shot Juliette an apologetic look. "It's fine. She doesn't have to tell us if she doesn't want to. Why don't we get dessert?"

She flagged down the server, who gave them the rundown of the day's dessert specials—all made fresh at the restaurant every morning.

They decided to split a piece of the mixed-berry cheesecake.

As soon as the server walked away to turn in their order, Kimberly said, "I'm curious about something. With the two of you living on opposite coasts, how will you and Owen make things work after you're married? Surely, one of you will relocate. Won't you?"

"We've talked about it," Juliette said. "We still have time to work it out."

"I know you will," said Tasha. "Would I be terrible if I were on team Tinsley Cove? I'd love nothing more than for you to move back so we could see each other more."

"I don't see how anyone could give up living the Hollywood dream," said Kimberly as she toyed with the spoon from her iced tea. "I mean, would you even be able to work if you moved back to Tinsley Cove?"

"I have well-established contacts in the film industry. I can still work," Juliette said, hoping she didn't sound defensive. "I can live anywhere I want as long as I go where the projects are filming."

"But that would mean that you and Owen would be

away from each other a lot," Kimberly said. "Wouldn't that be hard on a brand-new marriage?"

"That depends," Juliette said by way of hedging.

"Well, that wouldn't be good for a relationship."

What was she getting at?

Both Tasha and Juliette stared at Kimberly.

"I guess it's not so dissimilar to Richard working ninety hours a week," Juliette said.

"At least he comes home to my bed every night," Kimberly said, arching that perfectly shaped brow as if she were saying, *I'll see you one fiancé and raise you a sex life.* "I don't mean to overstep here, but let's face it, sex is important to a relationship—especially a new marriage. How will you manage if you're gone months at a time? I mean, even if Owen has his financial challenges, he's a hot guy. I'm just keeping it real."

Tasha said, "Yeah, but how much action is happening in your bed if Richard is exhausted from working all the time?"

Kimberly's mouth fell open.

"You guys," she said as if Tasha had just cut her to the quick. "First you make me feel bad about my ring. Now you're dooming my marriage before it even begins."

True to form, Kimberly could dish it out, but she couldn't take it.

Juliette bit back the words, *Just like you were dooming mine.*

My fake marriage.

A beat of awkward silence passed, and despite how much she adored Tasha, Juliette didn't want to move back to Tinsley Cove if it meant having to cross paths with Kimberly regularly.

Juliette gave herself a mental shake. The truth was, she wasn't moving back to Tinsley Cove. There would be no sex with Owen, because none of this was real.

Juliette was still processing that when Kimberly said, "I have to confess, after I learned that you worked in movies, I googled you, Jules."

Rather than saying something like, *That's weird,* or, *Stalker much?* or, *Don't call me Jules, Kimmy,* Juliette shot her a look that was meant to convey, *Okay. And?*

"I mean, even if you don't know Timothée Chalamet, you're living the Hollywood dream," Kimberly said. "I'll admit I'm jealous."

Kimberly held up her hands. "Only in the best possible way. I just don't understand how you could give up all of that, Juliette. Because you know Owen will never leave Tinsley Cove."

As Kimberly punctuated her point with a shrug, Juliette faltered a little bit, but she finally found her voice.

"Look, I can assure you we will be fine." She knew her tone sounded bitchy. "You don't need to worry about us, Kimberly."

"Frankly, it's not you I'm worried about," Kimmy said. "It's Owen. In hindsight, it's pretty clear now that Owen has always had a thing for you."

Wait, what? No he hasn't. It's called friendship.

"But you've evolved, Juliette," she continued. "I thought you'd moved on and outgrown him. That's why this whole thing—this whole engagement—is such a surprise."

The woman was a piece of work. Was it possible that a mean girl could get worse rather than seeing the error of her ways and growing up?

Juliette looked at Natasha for backup, but Tasha was staring at Kimmy in what appeared to be mortified disbelief.

Seemingly oblivious again, Kimmy had taken out her phone and was scrolling.

Enough was enough.

Juliette took her wallet out of her purse and pulled out her credit card. "I just saw the time, and I really need to get back to my mother. She's doing well, but she still isn't supposed to lift anything or raise her arms over her head."

Ignoring her, Kimberly asked, "Who is *this* hottie? I snapped a screenshot the other day when I was looking you up."

She handed her phone to Juliette. There was a picture of Juliette with Ed Day, her on-again, off-again producer boyfriend. They were on the red carpet before an awards show. Tall, with sandy curls and a body that looked as if it were sculpted from marble, it was true that Ed was good-looking, but lust didn't last. She hadn't thought about him since she'd told Owen why their relationship—if you could even call it that—had failed.

Juliette put the phone on the table face down and pushed it away. She didn't owe Kimmy an explanation.

"I mean Owen is hot, but this guy..." Kimmy let out a low, breathy whistle. "They don't make 'em like this in Tinsley Cove. You're really sure you want to trade in Ed Day, producer extraordinaire, for Owen McFadden, boy next door?"

Kimberly picked up the phone and showed it to Tasha as if the picture was proof positive before adding, "This guy is Justin Timberlake's doppelgänger. I mean, girl. I don't understand what's going on here. Something just doesn't add up. It just doesn't make sense."

Oh, no. Did Kimberly know about their agreement?

How could she know?

She couldn't.

Could she?

"Kimmy, why are you acting like this?" Tasha asked.

"Because I care about Owen, and I don't want him to be left holding the bag when she decides it's time to go back to her life in Los Angeles."

"Owen has gotten along perfectly fine all these years without you worrying about him, Kimberly," Juliette said. "I get the feeling that you're not so concerned about me leaving him as you are about me marrying him." She shouldn't have said it, but there it was. And she wouldn't stop there. "You need to understand that I love him, Kimberly, and we are getting married whether you like it or not."

"Yeah, well, we'll see about that." Kimmy's smile was chilling, and Juliette realized the entire restaurant was silent. Everyone was watching them.

As Juliette turned to find the server to pay her portion of the bill—she was not letting that woman pick up the tab for her lunch—she nearly ran into Dalton Hart.

"Good work, Kimberly," he said. "We'll call it a wrap."

Chapter Eight

Owen found the letter sandwiched between an old dog-eared football program and a calculous test that he had aced when he was a senior in high school.

Seated at his desk in his home office, he had been sorting through the box of mementos his mother had given him. He didn't realize what the envelope was at first, but when he saw Jules's name scrawled in faded blue ink on the front of the white letter-sized envelope, it all came flooding back.

Oh, wow.

His heart rate kicked up.

He sucked in a deep breath and leaned back in his chair, holding the envelope for a moment before examining it and seeing that it was still sealed.

No one had read it since he'd penned it more than thirteen years ago. All this time, it had been stashed in this box in his closet at his parents' house.

The box that his mother had brought him the morning he and Jules had announced their *engagement*.

Ironic.

He held the letter for a moment, afraid that opening it would be tantamount to letting a genie out of its bottle.

For that matter, maybe the genie had never been contained. The thought surprised him, and he pulled a letter opener from the pen holder on his desk, but before he could slice it open, someone rang the doorbell.

He glanced at the clock. It was probably Jules. She'd said she'd stop by after her lunch with the girls.

Rather than dropping the letter back into the box with all the other papers he needed to sort through, Owen opened the center desk drawer and slipped the envelope inside. He'd revisit it later, when he was alone.

In the meantime, it would be safe in the drawer.

"How did lunch go?" Owen asked after swinging open the door.

Before she answered, her bewildered look said it all.

"Uh-oh. Come in and tell me what happened."

Jules shook her head as she stepped into the foyer, keeping a respectable distance between them. "Kimberly was... Kimmy. Why did I think accepting her lunch invitation would be a good idea?"

"I wondered the same thing." He held up his hands. "But I figured you knew what you were doing."

"Next time, don't give me so much credit."

He was going to make a joke, but she looked so depleted, he didn't.

"Come here." He put his arms around her and pulled her close. He was relieved when she didn't recoil, but instead sank into him as if her body were deflating.

She felt so good in his arms, he could stay that way all day if that's what she wanted.

"Kimmy thinks I'm going to hurt you," she said into his shoulder.

Her words were muffled, and he wasn't sure he'd heard her right.

"What?" he asked, hating to break the spell to talk about Kimmy. Just as he'd suspected, Jules took a step backward, away from him.

"Kimmy thinks I'm going to hurt you," she repeated.

"Are you?" He smiled to let her know he was joking. Sort of joking.

When she didn't answer right away, he said, "And Kimmy's opinion matters why?"

She chuckled. "I know. That's what I kept asking myself all the way over here. What she thinks doesn't matter."

"Uh-huh, but I can see that it's bothering you." She looked wrung out, as if that woman had zapped the last ounce of her energy.

"Kimmy hasn't been part of my life for a long time," he said. "It's been years since I've seen her. I've gotten along just fine without her fighting my battles for me. Not that this is a battle. Don't let her bother you. Come on, let's go in here and talk about it."

He took her hand and led her into the living room. "Do you want a beer?"

She glanced at her watch. "No, thanks."

"Do you want something else? I'm not promising that a beer will cleanse your palate of Kimmy Ogilvie, but it might help."

She shrugged. "Sure, why not. It's five o'clock somewhere. And Ginny took Mom to the movies, and they're going to get a bite to eat afterward. I don't have to be anywhere. In fact, I might just hide out here if you don't mind."

"Make yourself at home," he said as he went into the kitchen, thinking that he loved her being there. She infused the place with a good energy that replenished him.

"Mi casa es tu casa."

He returned with two opened bottles and handed one to Jules.

"Thanks," she said and took a long pull. "While you were in the kitchen, I was thinking about something. Remember that time when Kimmy insisted we all call her KO?"

Owen squinted. "I don't. Sorry. It does sound like something she'd say, but I haven't held on to many memories of her except for how she used to suck all the oxygen out of the room. Obviously, that hasn't changed."

"How can you not remember her KO period? Those are her initials, of course, but she likened it to a KO in a boxing match. You know, as in knockout." Jules rolled her eyes then shook her head. "One day, she said, 'They don't call me KO for nothing,' and then she followed that up with a story that was so clearly bogus. She said that some guy had told her she was a total knockout and should shorten her name to simply KO."

"Wouldn't that be TKO, for total knockout?" Owen asked.

"I'm sure in Kimmy's mind it made sense."

"Don't tell me she brought up that story while you were having lunch."

"She didn't, but it kind of felt like she was threatening to knock me out if I hurt you. And I haven't gotten to the best part yet."

"Do tell," he said.

"I think she's joined the *Selling Sandcastle* cast."

"What? No she hasn't. I mean, I'm sure someone in my family would've warned me if that had happened."

Then again, he'd been so busy with work and arranging to meet with Richter that he hadn't seen them in days. Plus, he and Kimmy hadn't dated in years. So it wasn't as if she was a topic of conversation.

"Maybe she's not a full-fledged cast member, but today's lunch sort of felt like an ambush. One that she'd set up."

"What do you mean?"

"She quizzed me about you and the specifics of our relationship and engagement. Then Dalton Hart jumped out of the woodwork yelling, 'That's a wrap.' He was filming us, and afterward, the two of them seemed pretty chummy. Everything indicates that Kimmy was the one who organized the shoot. I think she was wearing a hidden microphone.

"Owen, it was awful." Jules bit her bottom lip and stared at her lap for a moment. When she finally looked up, meeting his eyes, she looked genuinely worried. "I may or may not have said some things to Kimmy that I regret. I'm sure everyone in the restaurant heard me when I doubled down on our engagement. By that time, the place was so quiet you could've heard a pin drop. Even over the echoing of my words. Then Dalton revealed himself and said, 'It's a wrap,' and everyone started clapping. They were eating this stuff up. I'm so embarrassed."

"You probably didn't say anything to Kimmy that she didn't deserve."

That show was the bane of his existence. It was starting to feel like the "Hotel California." He could quit anytime he wanted, but he would never be free of it.

"I'm sorry this keeps happening," Owen said. "I suppose Hart is free to record in public places, but I believe, unless you sign a release—you didn't, did you?"

"Absolutely not."

"Good. He can't use the footage. Maybe we should go to California and stay until the show wraps for the season. I doubt he'd chase us there."

"That's tempting, and since Mom is doing so well…" She trailed off, worrying her bottom lip. "So does the signed release requirement apply to you, too, then?"

"Unfortunately, it doesn't. I was looking over the contracts I signed for the seasons I was a cast member, and Hart slipped in a clause that says if I left the show, they could still use footage of me on future shows— new or from the archives."

"Oh, no." Jules buried her face in her hands for a moment. When she looked up, the ice-blue color of her eyes took his breath away.

"I know. It didn't seem important when we first signed on. I didn't go into this thinking it would become such an albatross. If my parents hadn't called for this to be the last season, I would probably hire an attorney to see if I could detach myself, but Hart thrives on conflict, and he would probably make it one of the central storylines. But just because I'm in it for the duration doesn't mean Hart can harass you."

He reached out and tucked a strand of blond hair behind her ear and then ran his thumb over her smooth cheek.

"It's going to be okay. I'm going to make a call to ensure it is."

He got his phone from his desk, found Hart in his contacts and called him.

"Owen, dude!" said Hart by way of greeting. "How's it hanging, my friend?"

Owen bit back the urge to say they weren't friends.

"What happened in Le Marais this afternoon?"

"*Ummm...* Can you be more specific? I'm sure there was a lot of steak fritesing and beef bourguignoning happening, but if you want a full menu, you'll have to pull it up on the website."

Smart ass.

"I think Juliette Kingsbury has made it clear that she doesn't want anything to do with your show. Are we going to have to get a restraining order to help you understand?"

He glanced at Jules. Those blue eyes were huge, but at least she was smiling now. It hit him that he would do anything to make her smile.

"Dude, don't be unreasonable," Hart said.

"Unreasonable is when someone asks you to leave them alone and you keep harassing them," Owen said. "So, let me make it perfectly clear. Juliette does not want to be filmed for *Selling Sandcastle*. Do you understand?"

"Loud and clear," Hart said and then disconnected the call.

"That should solve the problem." Owen set his phone down on the coffee table and looked at Jules, who looked more like herself now.

"Owen, thanks. Wow. Under normal circumstances, this would be the portion of the program where I told you I could stand up for myself, but clearly, these aren't normal times."

She glanced down at the ring on her left hand.

"It's kind of funny, because in my experience in the entertainment industry, we have to hire security to keep fans out. Dalton Hart seems to favor the sneak attack approach to getting people to be in his productions. It's just a bit weird to me. Although, Kimmy seemed to be all in for the show."

"I'm not trying to tell you what to do, but you might want to stay away from her while she's in town. Isn't she supposed to go back to Atlanta sometime soon?"

"Yes, except that she has offered to help Tasha and her mom throw the engagement party. She was asking about dates for the party, and I told her that we might be going out of town and we weren't sure when we'd be back. At least it was a valid reason to push off the party. I know it might get to the point where we run out of excuses—she was pushing pretty hard." Jules shrugged. "If it comes to that, I figured we would just get through it. She doesn't have to be a part of our life afterward."

Part of our life.

Our life.

He liked the sound of that. It made him feel warm inside.

But rather than asking her to define *our life,* Owen nodded. "Speaking of going out of town, I have some good news. Dan Richter called me back this afternoon."

"That's great. Did you set up a time to meet with him?"

"It's even better than that. He and his wife, China, have invited us to come out for the weekend and stay at his place in Cupertino."

"You said they invited *us.* I'm guessing that means you told him we were engaged." He couldn't quite read her expression.

"I didn't lead with it, but, yes, I did share the happy news."

She was quieter than he'd thought she would've been hearing the news that they had a reason to get out of town and away from the *Selling Sandcastle* quicksand.

After a few beats, she said, "It sounds promising. He wouldn't invite you to his home only to kick you to the curb. I'm so happy for you. Of course, I'll have to doublecheck with Ginny that she can stay with Mom over the dates that we'll be gone, but Mom is doing so well. And this is good. I'll call some of my industry contacts like you suggested and see what's going on—who's hiring. Maybe I can set up something for myself. You know, the bank account is getting a little low, and my share of the rent for the apartment in LA will be due…"

"Are you okay?" he asked. She was rambling, and she only did that when she was trying to pretend that she was fine but she wasn't.

"Of course I am. And, you know, if you seal the deal, we might be able to set an end date for our…for…umm… our arrangement." She waggled her left hand at him.

The first thing that came to his mind was that he wasn't in any hurry to wrap up the *arrangement*, as she'd put it. In fact, he hadn't even thought about an end date. He hadn't minded a single thing about it, from the excuse to be extra close to her to their families having dinner, to that kiss.

But he knew her life was in California.

"If you're short on cash, I can help, Jules."

"No, but thanks. I mean, I'm low, but I have a slush fund for rainy days like this. If you're in this industry and you're smart, you do that since the work can be sporadic."

She wrinkled her nose in that way that he'd always loved, but the smile that accompanied it didn't reach her eyes.

"You know I'm here for you if you need anything," he said.

"I know you are, and that's one of the reasons I love you so much."

His gut bunched and then did a strange flip thing that made him put his hand on his stomach.

"And I hope you know I'm here for you," she added. "Always."

"Then have dinner with me tonight," he said. "I was going to make some pesto pasta. Does that sound good?"

"It sounds delicious."

And just like that, the air between them changed and they'd found their equilibrium again.

"I always loved the movies because that was my way of shutting out the world and living a perfect, beautiful existence," she said, drying off the bunch of basil she'd just washed and setting it on the wooden cutting board. "Even if it was just for a couple of hours."

He gave the basil a rough chop. "How will your time in Tinsley Cove affect things?"

"I don't know," she said as she measured out the pine nuts for the pesto. "I told you I was seeing Ed Day, who is a producer."

And *more importantly…* "You said you guys broke up."

"We did."

She was quiet, and he worried that her silence meant that she regretted the split. Rather than ask that straight out, he came at it sideways.

"Do you want to talk about it?" he asked.

She poured the pine nuts into the blender. He added the basil and then turned toward her and leaned against the counter.

"I guess I should start by saying it's all for the best because of what my mom has been going through. I would've had to leave the production if I'd gotten the job. So…" She shrugged.

"Why didn't you get the job?"

Her eyes flashed with some kind of emotion that Owen couldn't decipher. Knowing that talking about Ed Day elicited such a reaction in her had his insides feeling a bit jagged.

"Originally, I did get the job. Ed offered me the showrunner position for the film *Argentine Tango*, but a couple of weeks later, after I mentioned I'd need to take off the weekend of Tasha's wedding, he told me it wouldn't work out. I know you don't get days off when you're filming on location, but I would've been gone for a weekend. If he'd wanted to, Ed could've covered for me. I wasn't going to miss Tasha's wedding. She's my oldest friend. I mean, you're my oldest friend. I've definitely known you longer. She's my oldest *girl* friend, but you're my *boo*."

Their gazed snared.

His brow arched and her eyes went wide. "I mean you're my… my bud. My buddy. You know what I mean."

She touched his arm, and he pushed back against the feeling that bud and buddy seemed like a consolation prize after tossing out boo and then taking it back.

"Then I learned that he'd fired me as showrunner because he'd hired Hazel Shine's niece instead. Hazel is starring in *Argentine Tango*. Apparently, her niece wants to get into film, and hiring the niece was a stipulation for Hazel taking the role."

Owen nodded because he didn't know what else to say. He was letting her vent, not trying to solve the situation for her.

"Everything would've been fine if I'd left it at that. You know, just let it go, but I couldn't. I told him that it felt personal because of our relationship. We'd been together over the course of two pictures. I know I shouldn't mix business and sex, but I didn't sign up to be a nun. I entered the relationship willingly. I didn't feel coerced or as if my sleeping with him was a prerequisite for getting the job. Where else am I supposed to meet men who understand that my job is demanding and takes me away for months on end? Because I told him it felt personal, he said we needed to end things. That's how we left it. I haven't spoken to him since. I'd like to think that he's professional enough to not blackball me over it. That wouldn't bode well for him, either, but we just left things in a bad place. I was hurt and mad. I mean, do you blame me?"

Before he could answer, she held up her hand. "Don't answer that. I learned a lesson. I shouldn't get involved with anyone on set. That is, if I can get another job."

She walked to the kitchen table and slumped down in a seat. "The truth is, I'm not sure I want another job in film."

Owen flinched. "Are your hurt feelings talking or do you really mean it?"

She shrugged. "I don't know. For as far back as I can remember, I wanted to work in film. But now, it's taking its toll on me. I'm thirty-one. I'm too old to be living hand to mouth and project to project. I feel like I should do something more serious. Everyone I know is settled in their lives and careers. Tasha is a CPA. Kimberly is a regional manager for a top cosmetics company. Not that I've ever thought of Kimmy Ogilvie as a life barometer. But even she is getting married and settling down. Here I am, after all these years, unsure if anyone will hire me and pretending to be engaged to my best friend."

There it was again. *Best friend.*

"You definitely deserve better than that, and if you're feeling restless, maybe it's time to make a change. Sometimes when you've been living what you thought was your dream, if you're not happy, you need to move on."

"It's not always that easy," she said.

"Believe me, I know." He thought about pointing out that he was in a similar boat, but the window hadn't completely closed for him. Instead, he found himself asking the question he dreaded.

"Are you still in love with Ed?"

She blinked at him then shook her head. "I never was in love with him."

An inexplicable sense of relief flooded through him. He didn't understand the feeling or know what to do with it. So he pushed it back into the corners of his mind.

"Then it's really over with him?"

"Yep. I'm done."

"Then maybe when we're in California, you should call him and see if you can chat. See if he has anything for you."

She gave an unenthusiastic one-shoulder shrug. "Maybe I will. Because even though I'm disenchanted with the industry, I don't know what else I would do."

They finished making dinner together, then enjoyed it on his patio, under the market lights he'd strung up in the spring. It was as if nothing strange had happened. After they'd cleaned up the kitchen, they made popcorn, opened another bottle of wine and went into the living room to watch a movie.

"What are you up for?" she asked.

"*The Shining* is streaming tonight," he said.

She made a horrified face. "No, thank you."

"Why? It's a classic. You should know that since you went to film school."

"It's a horror film. I don't do horror films. Don't work on them. Don't watch them."

She shuddered.

"Do you have a better suggestion?" he asked.

"How about a rom-com? We could watch *Jerry Maguire*."

He rolled his eyes.

"There are classics in that genre, too," she said. "Like *When Harry Met Sally* or *You've Got Mail*. Or we could go for a mainstream romance like *Breakfast at Tiffany's* or *Sabrina*."

He smirked, intending to yank her chain.

"Don't tell me you don't do romance." As soon as the words had crossed her lips, she covered her mouth with her hand. "Never mind. You don't have to answer that."

"Are you saying I don't do romance like you don't do horror movies, or are you talking about real-life relationships?"

He'd had the better part of a bottle of wine—enough to loosen him up...or get him in trouble.

"Both, right?" she answered for him. "Just like I had to deal with the horror show today at Le Marais."

"I'm thinking there's got to be a metaphor in our engagement situation that I could use to answer your question, but I've got nothing, which I'm blaming on the wine."

Luckily, she laughed, and he did, too.

He had enough sense to let it go at that.

After they settled on the couch, she held out her empty glass. He filled it halfway with wine and set the bottle on the coffee table.

"Okay, fine, we don't have to watch *The Shining*," he said. "I have no idea what else is streaming since I'd had my heart set on a little 'Here's Johnny'—that's a line from the movie, by the way."

"I figured as much, and now I feel bad crashing your movie night and changing the main feature."

"Don't worry about it," he said. "I'm sure we can find something else."

He should've asked her to hand him the remote, since it was on the end table on the other side of her. But he didn't. He reached across to grab it. As he was moving back to his place, he lost his balance and landed on top of her.

"Oh, hello, there." She bit her bottom lip.

Their gazes snared.

Maybe it was the wine, but mostly it was the need to taste her lips again—a need that had been growing since she'd laid that kiss on him on Jack and Tasha's wedding weekend.

If he just lowered his head a little bit—

"We can flip a coin," she said, breaking the spell.

He righted himself, giving her back her personal space.

"Flip a coin for what?" he asked.

"Heads, we watch *The Shining*. Tails, I get to pick the movie."

The coin landed on heads. He gave her an out, but she insisted that fair was fair. She said she knew how movies were made, that they were just stories acted out, and she was going to remind herself of that during the rough parts.

However, at the first appearance of the creepy twins beckoning Max to come play with them forever, she buried her face in Owen's shoulder. "I'm sorry. I can't watch this. It feels like it's damaging my soul."

He put an arm around her and pulled her tight. With his free hand, he groped for the remote and turned off the television.

"It's okay," he said. "You don't have to watch it."

The patio market lights were still on and shone in through the French doors that led out back. They cast a golden glow like candlelight. Jules nestled in closer, and for a moment, they sat there, snuggled together, holding on to each other as if they'd never let go.

He breathed in the clean, floral scent of her shampoo and that note that was uniquely Jules, and he knew he didn't want to let her go.

He wasn't sure who moved first, but suddenly, their mouths found each other.

She tasted like wine and honey and vaguely of the pesto she'd helped him make.

When they finally came up for air, she murmured, "I'd better go, because if I don't, I think we both know where this is leading."

"Would that be such a bad thing?" he asked.

"I don't know, would it? It might complicate things. Owen, I don't want to lose you because we lost ourselves tonight. I guess that's my one true thing for today."

She sat up and righted her blouse and smoothed her hair. In the dim light, her lips looked red and swollen, and he wanted to taste them again. No, he wanted to carry her to his bed and show her what a good thing making love to each other could be. He wanted to hold her all night and wake up with her in the morning.

But he would never force her to do something she didn't want to do.

He stood and offered her a hand, then pulled her into his arms again.

"My one true thing is not just for today," he said. "For as far back as I can remember, I've wanted this to happen."

He held her hand gently, reluctant to let her go, wanting her to know that this was him talking, not the wine

She smiled at him. It was so sultry that he almost came undone. "I'm going to let you sleep on that and make sure it still rings true tomorrow morning."

A week later, Owen steered the rental car onto Dan and China Richter's driveway.

"Is this the place?" he asked.

It had been an easy forty-five minute drive from San Francisco International Airport to their house in Cupertino.

Juliette checked the house number against the address on Owen's phone, which he'd programmed into the car's navigation system.

"This is it," she confirmed and pulled down the vanity mirror behind the sun visor to check her hair and makeup.

"Interesting," he said. "I thought a tech mogul like Richter would live in a palace."

They both leaned forward and peered at the *nuevo* mission-style house, with its white stucco walls and dark brown wooden garage door and trim. The spacious front porch was made of limestone. It led to double front doors made out of ornate dark brown metal. It could've been a smaller cousin to Owen's parents' house, only it was half the size and was plunked down in an ordinary, tree-lined middle-class neighborhood between two split-level houses that appeared to have been built in the seventies or eighties.

"Listen to you, snobby," she said. "It looks like a nice house. In fact, it looks like new construction. Knowing property values out here, I'm sure whatever they paid for it would buy a palace somewhere."

"I didn't mean it wasn't a nice house." His voice had an edge to it.

"I know you didn't. I was just joking with you."

She reached out and took his hand. The same way he'd held hers when their flights had taken off because he knew how much she hated to fly.

"Don't be nervous. Dan Richter is going to love you."

Now she wanted to give him that same reassurance he'd given her. Just as he'd steadied her pre-takeoff jitters and silently assured her that the plane was not going to go down in flames, his career wasn't going to crash and burn, either.

Only she wasn't going to say that out loud. Just as

he hadn't talked about plane crashes when they took off. No one needed to hear things like that. So, as they always had during challenging times, they wordlessly communicated with a look, a touch and something like telepathy that assured, *This might be tough, but I'll be your shelter.*

The house's front doors opened, and a tall, reed-thin woman with perfect blond hair that looked like it had been naturally bleached by the sun stepped out onto the porch. She was wearing a cute yellow-and-blue boho-style dress that hit her tanned thighs midway, showing off flawless legs. She was barefoot, and her hair hung down her back in perfect beach waves. She looked effortlessly gorgeous, like a mermaid who'd traded in her scales and flippers for the California life.

The blonde woman waved to them from the porch.

"That must be Dan's wife," said Owen. "Are you ready for this?"

"Of course. And you are going to do great."

She wasn't sure what came over her, but she leaned in and placed a whisper of a kiss on his lips. The memory of the kiss they'd shared a week ago at his place made her body sing. She longed to deepen the kiss and see where it led today, but she couldn't with their hostess for the weekend standing on the porch ready to greet them.

"*Mmm*, that was nice." Owen's voice was low and raspy, and she could imagine him thinking the same thing.

She imagined them telling China Richter that they'd be back in and hour…or in the morning—

Wait. No. What was wrong with her?

As if reminding herself, she said, "It doesn't hurt to get into character."

"You play the role well. Let me know if you'd like to practice some more. I'm here for you."

He smiled and raised a brow. The offer sent hot, electric frissons coursing through her, pooling in personal, sensitive places.

"Don't make promises you don't intend to keep."

"Try me," he said.

"Maybe I will." She let herself out of the car because if she knew what was best for her—best for them—she shouldn't keep pushing the envelope.

"Hello! Hello!" the woman called. "You must be Owen and Juliette. I'm China Richter, Dan's wife. I'm so happy you're here. Please come in and make yourself at home. Congratulations on your engagement. Dan shared the happy news. I'm a sucker for a wedding. So, I hope we'll get an invitation."

"Absolutely," said Owen as he grabbed their bags and followed the women inside.

They stopped in the foyer, and Juliette noticed that the house was much larger than it had appeared from the driveway.

"Your home is lovely, China."

They chatted for a few minutes. Then China said, "Why don't we take those bags right up to your room? That way, if you want to freshen up before dinner, you can," China said. "The elevator is right over here. You two can ride up. Since there won't be room for all three of us and the luggage, I'll take the steps."

"No, you two ride up with the bags," Owen offered. "I'm happy to take the stairs."

"I won't hear of it," China said. "I'm sure you're exhausted after your long flight. Besides, I need the exercise anyway."

China was so thin, she looked like she needed a cheeseburger and a big plate of fries, Juliette thought, and then mentally admonished herself for having such uncharitable thoughts. But all thoughts of China Richter soon disappeared when Juliette and Owen stepped into the close space of the elevator and the doors closed. As the lift lurched to a start, they were pressed against each other, breast to chest. His arms went around her.

"You want to get in some practice?" he murmured, gazing down at her with hooded eyes.

"I don't know. If you get me started, you might not be safe inside this box with me."

"I might be willing to take my chances."

That same heat that had flooded her body in the car pulsed through her again. She thought he was going to kiss her, but the elevator stopped, allowing them a moment to gather their wits. Still, Owen didn't take his arms from around her right away.

They stepped out of the lift onto an open loft area. Needing to get ahold of herself, Juliette walked over to the wall and peered down into the living area where they'd just been.

"I've put you two in the suite at the end of the hall," China said as she moved toward a corridor on their left. "Other than our room, it's the best bedroom in the house. Two other couples—Liza and Tom Faraday and Emily and Phil Crandal—will be joining us this weekend, too. Liza and Tom are staying out in the guesthouse. Emily and Phil will be in the annex. You two have this wing to yourself this weekend."

China lifted a brow, and the corner of her full mouth turned up in a suggestive smile.

Then she held up her left arm. The blousy sleeve of her dress fell away to reveal a Cartier Tank watch. "Let's see… It's almost five o'clock now. The others should be here in about an hour. Dan will be home by then, too. That should give you some time to relax. Cocktails are at seven. Dinner is at eight. How does that sound?"

"It sounds like a plan," Owen said.

"Wonderful," China chimed as they followed her into a large bedroom with a king-size bed and a sitting area. "You'll find water, wine and some light snacks in the refrigerator, which is in the armoire. You should have everything you need in the bath. If you need anything else, please don't hesitate to let me know. Please, make yourselves at home."

Then she breezed out, leaving Owen and Juliette alone staring at the king-size bed.

Suddenly, all the practice they'd been joking about seemed very real.

"I can sleep on the couch if it would make you more comfortable," Owen said

"It's not like we haven't slept together before," she said. "*Slept* being the operative word. When we were in high school, we fell asleep plenty of times when we were watching movies. And it's not like I haven't seen you naked before."

He flinched and smiled. "When have you seen me naked? Not that I'd care if you had."

"When we used to skinny-dip in your swimming pool."

"We were two years old, Jules. I don't think that counts."

"Oh, I don't know." She raised her brows and made a show of looking him up and down. "I think it does."

"You letch," he teased. "If you were still into skinny-dipping, you should've said something last week when we had dinner. I would've been happy to accommodate."

Again, her mind went back to that wine-fueled kiss.

Now she wondered what would've happened if she hadn't made such a hasty exit.

He had certainly grown up and filled out nicely, with those shoulders and chest and the flat abs that tapered into a slim waist. His naturally athletic body had developed through years of swimming and surfing.

I wouldn't mind seeing you naked now.

She felt heat start in her cleavage and threaten to blossom upward. She turned away, pretending to need something in her suitcase.

"I think I'll take a bath. Do you need in the bathroom first?"

"No, I'm good," he said, checking out the refreshments in the armoire. "Go ahead. Oh, hey, there's a bottle of Veuve Clicquot in the fridge. Why not take a glass of champagne in for your bath?"

"They gave you champagne? I think that's a good sign."

"They gave *us* champagne," he said and popped the cork. "Remember, we're getting married."

As he handed her the glass of bubbly, her heart squeezed and a little voice inside her surprised her when it said, *If only it were true.*

Chapter Nine

By all accounts, the night had gone well.

The five-course Moroccan dinner prepared by the Richters' chef had been delicious. China had been a gracious hostess, leading the lively conversation so that everyone was engaged and included. Dan had seemed genuinely happy to see Owen and meet his fiancée.

The electricity between Juliette and Owen had been palpable, like an invisible, but very real, cord connecting the two of them. When they were next to each other, they were touching. When they weren't next to each other, each was aware of the other, their eyes meeting across the room, silently communicating and stoking this fire that had sparked that night at Owen's house and had intensified as each day progressed.

Tonight, it seemed as if the fire would consume them.

As the night slipped away, pushing them closer to that king-size bed in their suite upstairs, Juliette thought she might explode with want.

Finally, the party broke up, and Owen and Juliette headed toward the elevator.

"Here we are again, in this small space," Owen said

after the door opened and they stepped inside. "And I'm not feeling the least bit unsafe with you. In fact, all night, all I could think about was being in here with you."

"Great minds." She angled her body toward him.

The doors closed, and he pushed the button for the second floor and turned to her.

His starched white shirt was a gorgeous contrast to the rich olive tone of his skin. She longed to unbutton it and reveal more skin.

As if reading her lusty thoughts, he pulled her close. "I don't know, maybe I'd better hold on to you."

She locked her hands around his neck and wondered what he meant by that.

Hold on to me?

For how long?

The duration of the ride?

The weekend?

Forever?

As the elevator carried them up, Owen bent down and teased gentle kisses on her cheekbones, on that delicious spot behind her ear, trailing his way down until he'd reached the delicate indent between her neck and collarbone. He brushed her blond hair to one side to give himself better access to her neck.

She ran the flat of her palm down his torso, stopping at the waistband of his pants.

"You are making me crazy," he murmured into her ear.

He was making her stupid with want. Luckily, the elevator stopped and the doors opened before things went further, as if the universe was telling her this was her last chance to pull herself together.

To not cross that line.

But why not?

She'd spent her whole life not crossing lines, accommodating everyone else so she could get jobs that lasted a few months and then put her back at square one.

Where had that gotten her?

It had relegated her to playing the minor roles. Never the leading lady.

Not in work.

Not in her own life.

Not in anyone else's life.

For once, she was doing something for herself because she wanted to. She wanted him and she had for a long time.

Things had gone so well at dinner that it was clear that Dan was in, that he and Owen would sign the agreement. When they did, and a reasonable amount of time passed, she could call off the engagement. She would be in California. Owen would be in Tinsley Cove.

If not now, when? Because Owen was a strong, sexy handful of a man, and if she didn't do this now—before the clock struck midnight and their coach turned back into a pumpkin—she knew she would regret it for the rest of her life.

They spilled out of the lift. After the doors closed, Owen pulled her into his arms.

She pushed all other thoughts out of her head and gave into the moment, meeting him halfway as he leaned in and covered her mouth with his.

His kiss was tender at first, transporting her to a heady place that crashed through the boundaries of friendship.

He tasted vaguely of the wine he'd had tonight at dinner and something else, something delicious. Something that she'd craved since that night at his house, since that night at the cocktail party before the wedding, since that night on his front porch when he'd kissed her. Actually, she'd wanted this long before then—since that night, all those years ago, when he'd kissed her on his front porch after the graduation party.

She moved in closer, opening her mouth, inviting him in.

A muffled growl sounded from deep inside him. He deepened the kiss and pulled her flush against him.

She was vaguely aware of the sound of clinking dishes and people moving around downstairs. The sound of the Richters' staff cleaning up after the dinner party.

They'd better take this to their room before things went too far.

But China had assured them that they had this wing of the house all to themselves.

With that, her mind went foggy and the only thing she was aware of was the feel of his lips, those capable—no, those *accomplished*—lips on hers. She fisted her hands into his collar, wanting to eliminate any space between them.

He was so darn good at this. So good at invading her personal space and making the rest of the world go away as he intuitively touched her just the way she wanted to be touched. They were good together in this fantasy world they'd created. Right now, for this night, she didn't have to think beyond that.

Juliette didn't care about anything but this single moment suspended in time where nothing else existed but the two of them and this growing need that was threatening to devour her.

Her fingers were in Owen's hair, and his hands were moving over her—starting at her shoulders and tracing their way down her body, as if he was memorizing her every curve and angle. His touch felt so good on her body, and she wanted to commit this moment to memory so she could remember it forever. Especially when he cupped her bottom and aligned their bodies perfectly together.

Then Owen's hands went exploring, this time venturing upward, grazing the sides of her breasts, lingering there for a moment and then working their way back down to tug loose her blouse from her skirt.

His hands glided underneath her blouse. Juliette moved back ever so slightly to grant him access. She gasped when his fingers deftly slid beneath the satin and lace of her bra and found her sensitive nipples, making a thousand stars shoot through the obsidian sky of her mind's eye.

"Let's go to our room," she said breathlessly.

He answered her by deepening the kiss, breaking it only to scoop her up and carry her down the hall and over the threshold.

"You're such a gentleman."

"I'm glad you think so because the things I want to do to you are decidedly ungentlemanly."

"I can't wait."

Owen carried her down the hallway. Once they were inside the room, he kicked the door shut and carried her over to the bed where all the innuendoes had started.

"I guess you're not going to sleep on the couch," she said.

"Who said anything about sleeping?"

He didn't bother to turn on the lights, simply lowered himself onto the bed beside her.

He unbuttoned her blouse, lifting her just enough to slide it off and toss it away.

He must've known how much she wanted him, because everything about him was hard with arousal. And yet his hands were gentle as he found the clasp of her bra and deftly opened it with two fingers. She let it fall to the ground, joining the pile of other things that only got in the way. It wasn't her nakedness that gave her pause as much as it was her emotional vulnerability. Could he read the desire in her eyes as clearly as she could read it in his? He put her at ease when he ran his hands over her body, which was aching for his touch. As he worked his magic, she found herself inhaling a ragged breath a second before a low moan escaped her lips.

His hands just seemed to instinctively know what to do to make her body sing.

She didn't try to control her response; she let herself go, allowing her reaction to come spontaneously and unselfconsciously.

He made quick work of getting rid of her skirt. Then he slid his hands upward, along her thigh to her hip, until his finger caught the delicate lace edge of her panties. In one swift move, he tugged them down and helped her out of them.

"Who's making who crazy now?" she whispered.

"Yeah? You haven't seen anything yet."

Owen couldn't get enough of her.

Even so, as she propped herself up on her elbow and her fingers began working the buckle of his belt, he put his hand over hers to press pause.

"Are you sure about this?" he asked.

"I am. Are you?"

"I've never been more sure about anything in my life," he said. "I just don't want you to have any regrets."

She blinked, then looked away.

For a moment, he was afraid she was going to pull away from him. It would take every ounce of strength he possessed to remove himself, but if that's what she wanted, then...

"I want this, Owen. I think we've spent way too much time overthinking things. It's time we went with the flow."

He smiled and ran his hand down her bare thigh. "Went with the flow, huh? Are you sure that's what you want?"

"A very sexy wise man once said, 'I've never been more sure about anything in my life.'" She smiled and traced the closed zipper of his fly with her finger. "So, yeah."

He leaned in and kissed her, tentatively at first, giving her one last chance to back away, but she dug her fingers into the hair on the back of his head and pulled his mouth soundly to hers.

With Owen's lips on hers, Juliette reached between them, unbuttoned his shirt and then finished unbuckling his belt. He leaned back slightly, giving her just enough access to work the zipper on his trousers. After that, he took care of the rest; with a push of one hand, his pants and his boxers fell away, eliminating the final barriers between them.

He answered with a throaty growl, grasping the crook of her knee and drawing her leg up and around him. He lifted her so that she could encircle him with both legs.

From the moment he'd realized that girls were different than boys, Juliette had owned his soul. Now, she was in his arms.

They would be perfect together. He wanted to get inside her—figuratively and literally—and figure out what it was about her that rendered him so weak in her presence.

Like anything that had proven to be a challenge, he wanted to conquer her, to possess her, but the truth was, she already possessed him.

Everything about her—that lithe body, those blue-blue eyes, that mouth that drove him crazy—set his senses on fire.

So many nights he'd thought of her, but he'd distracted himself with business or other women because he'd been sure that he'd never be with her. Not like this. He'd never feel her touch. Never get the chance to know her so intimately.

Now here they were.

* * *

Juliette straddled Owen and ran her fingers across the smooth, taut muscles of his bare chest and shoulders. Spellbound, she let her hands discover him, feeling every muscled ridge, savoring the glorious treasure of his body, savoring the hot, smooth manliness of him.

That's when she saw the tattoo on his left shoulder. In the dim amber light she could make out the shape... like an abstract ocean wave. That made sense because of his love for surfing.

When did he get a tattoo?

It could've been anytime, because when was the last time she'd seen him like this? Well, she'd never seen him like *this*, but she had seen him without a shirt on.

But the more she looked at the design, the more it looked like an *O* and a *J* woven together to form a breaking ocean wave.

The words were on her lips to ask him about it, but then he flipped her over so that she was on her back and he was on top of her.

As he kissed her, she reached between them and took the hard length of him into her hands. His head dropped back and his whole body stiffened, and he let out a measured breath that heartened and aroused her even more.

"If you keep touching me like this, I won't be any good to you. There's so much more I want to do with you."

With him, she wanted to do things she'd never done, had never wanted to do with anyone else. She wanted him to see her pleasure in doing them with him. She raised her hips and guided him to where she needed him the most.

"Wait… Wait a minute," he said breathlessly, putting space between them. "We can't—"

"Wait—what? Why?" Yes, they most certainly could, and she had no idea why they were stopping. "What's wrong?"

"I know I should've thought ahead, but honestly, I didn't think we'd end up here. Like this. Not that I don't want to. You have no idea how much I want this—but what about birth control? And *health*. I know it's a mood killer to talk about that right now. Like this. I'm sorry, but I have to be honest with you because I'm *safe,* if you know what I mean, but we both have to be safe."

He grimaced and fell onto his back, and all of a sudden, she realized what he was saying.

"I have good news," she said, propping herself onto her elbow. "Remember how China said we'd find everything we'd need in the bathroom?"

His eyes widened.

"She really did think of everything."

"She really is the hostess with the mostest," he said through a lopsided smile. His thick dark hair fell over one eye, and when she pushed it back off his face, a possessive tenderness blossomed inside her.

Again, she smoothed her palms over those masculine shoulders of his. God, how they drove her crazy. His skin was hot and his muscles were hard. His body was smooth, except for a patch of dark hair in the center of his chest. Just enough, she thought. Just enough to be sexy and manly and make her want him so bad that she was throbbing. She had to summon every ounce of self-control to keep from moving her center down just a few inches so that she could take him right now.

They were going to make love.

It was going to happen.

So, yeah, *this* was going to happen. And right now, she couldn't think of anything she wanted more.

The heady realization racked Juliette's body with shudders. Right now, it seemed terribly romantic. Lying here with him, naked and vulnerable, allowing him past her personal barriers, there was no place to hide when you opened yourself up to someone like that. And that was…okay.

So was the way he seemed to take possession of her with his eyes. Their chemistry was explosive. She loved everything he did. Everything he said. Everywhere he touched…

Moments—or maybe it was hours—later, as he positioned himself over her, it all became clear.

She wanted to tell him that she was falling for him—that she *had* fallen for him. *Hard.*

But she was afraid that if she did, it might break the spell, or even worse, if she spoke, she might wake up from this lovely dream.

Finally, after the touching and kissing built to a fever pitch, he thrust into her, filling her with his bulk and heat. She gripped his shoulders tightly, matching him thrust for thrust. His forehead glistened with sweat, and his biceps bulged. Their gazes locked, and he built a strong rhythm, which got faster and faster until it felt as though they were two souls merging into one.

Just as she went over the edge, a guttural growl sounded from Owen's throat. Then, very slowly, ever so tenderly, he lowered his body to cover hers.

They lay there like that for a long time before he turned over on his back next to her, pulling her in close.

"What's this?" She gently traced the tattoo with her fingernail.

"It's the logo for my company, SmartScape," he said.

A thousand thoughts rushed her brain.

She wanted to ask him who designed it and if that really was a *J* and *O* that she saw, but the more she looked at it, the more she saw two *S*'s interwoven to make the wave shape.

Plus, there was a heavier question lurking in the back of her mind: *What now...for us?*

Everything had changed.

They were returning to Tinsley Cove the day after tomorrow. They wouldn't be able to spend much time together before that, because Owen had plans to play golf with Dan and the other guys.

China had organized a brunch for the wives.

Juliette refused to get needy and clingy now. That was a sure way to ruin things. She had known that going into last night.

The only problem was that she hadn't counted on feeling quite so vulnerable after she finally got what she wanted.

Lying here with this beautiful, beautiful man in a private wing of this fairy-tale house with a staff that catered to their every need, it had been too easy to lose herself in the role she was playing. She and Owen weren't really engaged. They weren't even a couple. They were pretending to be together as a means to an end, and it looked as if that end was in sight.

This was pretend.

She reached out and ran her hand across Owen's chest as if the warmth of his naked body lying there next to her might prove something different.

The truth remained that he had made her no promises, except that they would make a clean break once her mother was well and his deal was signed and sealed.

But what now, Owen?

As if reading her mind, he said, "Did you hear back from any of your film contacts?"

She'd called Ed and a few other people who'd been working on *Argentine Tango* to see if the cast and crew were back in town, but she hadn't heard back from anyone. She shook her head and smoothed the area of the bedsheet that lay between them and then raked her fingers through her bedhead hair.

"I'll follow up with them tomorrow."

He turned over onto his side and propped himself up on his elbow. His beard was starting to come through, and with his tattoo and mussed hair, he looked a little dark and dangerous.

And sexy as hell.

"I'm still open to changing our return fight if you want to drive down to Los Angeles and see what's what."

She shrugged.

"I don't know. If I don't hear from anyone, there'd be no sense in going all the way down there. I'd be better off figuring out what's what over the phone when we get back to Tinsley Cove. I guess I'm not quite ready to get back to real life."

He reached out and smoothed a strand of hair off her forehead. His gaze was sexy—dark and intense. She felt herself melting like beeswax in his hands, especially when he trailed a thumb from her bottom lip, over the hollow at the base of her throat, through the valley of her cleavage. Then he splayed his hand possessively over her belly, unleashing a troop of butterflies that trailed a warm glow through her body. The thought of staying like this both excited and terrified her. The business deal was as good as signed and sealed for him. As soon as she was sure her mom was well enough to be on her own, Juliette would return to California and they would break up.

Tonight, she had allowed herself to get lost in the fantasy of it all.

"This has been...fabulous," she said. "But tomorrow—"

He pressed a gentle finger to her lips.

"Tomorrow is another day," he said. "Right now, it's still tonight. Let's live in the moment."

She wanted this, too. It should've been so easy to just extend their stay and prolong the inevitable, but something was holding her back.

The coffee house was located just outside of Cupertino. It was a funky little shop that looked like a throwback to the 1970s. The walls were painted avocado green. Spidery philodendrons were suspended from the ceiling in macramé plant hangers. Patrons on laptop computers sat in rattan chairs at glass tables. Others reading books lounged on brown plaid sofas and over-stuffed chairs. The scent of dark coffee beans, which a sign proudly proclaimed were roasted on-site, hung in the air.

She spied Ed sitting at a table, scrolling on his phone.

That morning, after Owen had left to play golf with the guys, Ed had called and said that he'd just gotten back to LA. When she told him she was in Cupertino, he'd offered to drive up and see her.

"That's a long way," she'd said. "You don't have to do that."

"If I leave now, I can be there by two," he'd said. "Does that work for you?"

It did work. It gave her plenty of time for China's brunch. After that while the other three women sunned themselves by the pool, she begged off, opting to *visit a friend*.

As she approached Ed's table, he looked up and smiled. "There you are." He stood and opened his arms. She hesitated for a split second before hugging him.

Even after what happened with Owen last night, Juliette had no reason to feel guilty. She and Owen were not a couple. She was determined that last night would not change a thing between them.

"How did the filming of *Argentine Tango* go?" she asked.

"Good. Good. All of the location shots went smoothly. We are regrouping and meeting at the studio on Monday. We will get the final interior shots then. What are you doing? Are you back in California?"

"Well, clearly, yes." She held up her hands palms up with the intent of good-natured ribbing.

Ed smiled and rolled his eyes. "Yes, clearly, you're here now, but, are you are back in California for good? And what are you doing in Cupertino, of all places?"

That was a good question, and she wasn't quite sure how to explain it. Since entering into this agreement with Owen, she had been hyperaware of every single non-truth, even the slightest little white lie that had been meant to protect those she cared for. It was best to just keep it simple. Stick to the simple facts.

"I am here with a friend who is in town on business."

It was the truth.

Ed looked confused.

"How is your mom doing?"

She'd almost forgotten that she'd told him about her mom, but she had. In the wee hours of the morning, the night that her mom had been admitted, Juliette had texted Ed because she needed somebody to talk to. He had been filming in Spain, so his response had been short and sweet.

"She is still recovering. A friend is staying with her while I I'm here. But I'm going home tomorrow."

"Any idea when you'll be back?" he asked. "In LA?"

"Not sure. I mean, it shouldn't be much longer. I'll know more when I get home. I mean, when I get back to Tinsley Cove. Mom has a doctor's appointment, and he will give us the assessment."

"Well, I hope she gets a clean bill of health. Selfishly, I miss you in LA. I want you to come back."

He missed her? Despite the casual way they used to approach their relationship, there had been times of weakness when she had longed to hear him say he missed her. It was happening now, and yet the words felt flat. Her mind kept going back to Owen. The way he had looked at her. There had been a time when she would've given anything to have Ed Day look at her the way he was looking at her now, but now, it just made her uncomfortable.

She noticed he had already gotten coffee.

Rather than comment about him missing her or banter with him like she would have with Owen, she couldn't find the words.

Really, what was she supposed to say?

"I'll be right back. I'm going to get some coffee. Any recommendations?"

Ed shrugged. "I'm just a regular coffee kind of guy. Black and strong. I don't go for the froufrou."

Once again, with Ed, she was on her own. Even if it was just a coffee recommendation.

In line to order her coffee, the thumb of her left hand rubbed the band of the engagement ring. She had forgotten all about it. Thank goodness Ed hadn't noticed.

Then again, Ed seemed to only have an eye for detail when it came to film. She switched the ring from her left hand to her right. If he did notice it, she was certain that he would not say anything about it. She ordered a cappuccino and brought the ceramic mug to the table, where Ed had returned his focus to his phone. As she sat down, he finished typing out a text and then turned his phone face down on the table.

"How did things go on location?" she asked as she slid into the chair across the table from him.

Ed filled her in on the six weeks they'd been abroad. It sounded pretty run-of-the-mill, except that he hadn't mentioned Hazel Shine's niece, the woman for which they'd thrown her over. Finally, Juliette got tired of waiting for Ed to mention her.

"How did Hazel Shine's niece work out?"

Ed blinked at her as if he wasn't sure what she meant. "Sally? She's a good kid."

"Did Sally do a good job?"

Ed looked away and slurped his coffee. Did he look guilty?

Oh my gosh, he looks guilty. Did he sleep with her?

Would he sleep with the niece of the principal actor? Was he that dumb?

"Oh, well, you know. She wasn't you. There's a steep learning curve when you're inexperienced, but she's settling into the job."

The funny thing was, Juliette realized she didn't care. Juliette wasn't the first showrunner that Ed Day had had an affair with, and Hazel Shine's niece would not be the last. As long as Ed was producing films, he would find pleasure in the arms of someone on the set for the duration of a picture, and it would probably be whoever happened to be the showrunner.

She died a little inside. Not because of any love lost for Ed but because it felt so dirty. Like she was expendable, an interchangeable part.

Because of that, she took a great big emotional step back as she listened to Ed catch her up on the comings and goings of people they both knew in the industry.

Just as the conversation had started to wind down, Juliette's phone rang. She fished it out of her purse and saw that the call was from her roommate, Ingrid. She decided to let it go to voicemail.

She would call her back on her way home. Juliette had been trying to get in touch with her since she and Owen had firmed up the plans for their trip, but despite the many voicemails Juliette had left, this was the first time Ingrid had called her back.

She'd waited this long to call. She could wait a little bit longer for Juliette to call her back. Besides, after Ed had so unceremoniously unhired Juliette from *Argentine Tango*, Ingrid had decided the man was scum. Despite the fact that Juliette did not need anyone fighting her battles for her, Ingrid had promised Juliette that the first chance she got, she was going to give Ed a piece of her mind.

So, yeah, Ingrid could wait a little longer. Especially because Juliette was going to have to get on the road back to Cupertino. Owen and the guys should be back from playing golf soon. A ping of guilt stabbed her right in the solar plexus. If she got back to the Richter's house before Owen got home, would she need to tell him that she had driven thirty miles to meet her ex-boyfriend for coffee?

Of course she would. Her main reason for meeting Ed was to see if he knew of any productions that would be hiring in a month or so.

She'd asked him, and he'd said, "As a matter of fact, I am going to work on a new project in four or five months. I'd love to work with you again."

He reached out and put his hand over hers. "I've missed you, Juliette."

It was interesting and sad at the same time that before she had gone home to Tinsley Cove, hearing that Ed had missed her, that he wanted her for a job and, of course, everything else that implied, would have made her day. Now it made her feel... Nothing. Of course, if she did take the job, it didn't mean that she had to resume their...relationship? Affair? Whatever it was that she and Ed had been doing on-again, off-again for the past two years.

It was over now.

It made her feel a little sad because it was like discovering that you had no appetite for a dish that had once been your favorite food.

It was weird.

She didn't have to sort it out now, but something inside told her it was well and truly over with Ed.

He walked her out to her car. "I'll give you a call once I know more about the project," he said. "As far as I'm concerned, the job is yours, if you want it."

He leaned in and tried to kiss her, but she turned her head and his lips landed on her cheek.

He raised his brows in surprise, but then smiled as if he understood.

"Goodbye, Ed. It was good to see you."

Juliette watched Ed walk away. When he reached his car, he didn't look back. He simply drove off.

This is how it ends. It's okay with me.

Before she started the car, Juliette listened to the voicemail Ingrid had left earlier.

"Hey, hey, hey, girlfriend! I am so sorry it's taken me so long to return your call, but I have a very good reason. Are you sitting down? You won't believe it, but Harry and I eloped! We were in Vegas, and we saw one of those cute little Elvis chapels, and we looked at each other and said, 'Why not?' So we bit the bullet and got married. Can you believe it?

"Now, for the not so fun news, but I know you'll understand. I didn't want to say this over voicemail, but I'm not sure when you and I are going to be able to talk again since you're traveling and I am in and out, but I know you're concerned about your mom and you want to spend some time with her in North Carolina. I hope she's doing well. You have been an ideal roommate, and I love you for that. However, as newlyweds, Harry and I really want some space of our own. So, you'll need to start looking for another place. I hope you understand. I said to Harry, 'Juliette is such a good friend. I know she'll understand.' Talk soon."

Great. Now she really didn't have anything in LA to return to—well, once she collected her things. So where did that leave her? The little fantasy life she had created with a certain someone came to mind. But could it ever be more than just that, a fantasy?

Chapter Ten

For their last night together, China had arranged for the four couples to have an elegant picnic on the beach. Even though the closest beach was about an hour away.

China and Dan had provided a car to drive them to and from the picnic, which had been exquisite. They had dined on fresh seafood on a trestle table set up under twinkle lights that had been strung from posts set up right on the beach.

It was magical.

Now dinner was over and everyone was lingering over the last of the wine. Owen saw it as an opportunity for him and Juliette to excuse themselves for a few moments, before the cars were set to drive them back to Dan's house. Owen had something he wanted to tell her.

Earlier that day, while Owen was playing golf, she'd texted and told him she'd driven to meet Ed. Even though he knew he didn't have any right to be jealous, he was feeling possessive.

Okay, he *was* jealous.

She had gotten back to the house with little time to spare before they'd taken off for the beach, and she'd seemed a little distant. She hadn't wanted to talk about

Ed, using the excuse that she needed to hurry and get ready for dinner.

Because of that, Owen had held back on telling her about his day on the golf course with Dan and had gone downstairs to give her some space.

Now, as they walked, he wanted to fill her in on the news: Dan had committed to investing in SmartScape Technologies.

"Dan is on board with SmartScape." Her eyes locked on his, but they were unreadable. *Did something happen during her meeting with Ed?* "A great deal of why he changed his mind has to do with you, Jules."

"Don't be ridiculous," she said. The wind blew her curls into her eyes and she brushed them away. "This is all you, Owen. You did the work. You didn't give up. You made it happen."

But it was because of her encouragement and clear-headedness. It was because of her support. She believed in him. She'd been absolutely right about telling Dan about *Phrase Fusion*. At one point on the golf course, Owen thought Dan was going to ask for his autograph. He'd been that impressed. He'd said his wife was obsessed with the game and played it every day.

What Owen had thought of as a fluke, which could've been a strike against him, this investor, who was now his friend, had considered a stroke of genius—that was Dan's word. Not Owen's.

So, this was all because of Jules. Life just seemed better when they were together.

He didn't want it to end.

"I'm going to tell you something that's true. Or at

least it's always been true for me. I'm counting on you to not judge me or make me feel bad for sharing this, because it's important and it's real. The most important thing is I don't want this…" He moved his hands in a circle in a way meant to be the fake engagement and the speculative marriage proposal—and the confession he was about to make.

"You know you can tell me anything," she said. "We made it through you becoming the cool kid after your parents moved at the start of high school. We survived the Kimmy years, when she wanted nothing more than for you to abandon me. You didn't, thank you very much. Our friendship survived college and me moving to Los Angeles. I can't think of anything you could say or do that would make me think less of you."

"Okay." He inhaled sharply and blew out the breath in a slow, steady, measured exhale. Then he squeezed his eyes shut and rubbed the back of his neck. Finally, he looked her straight in the eyes.

"I love you, Jules. Always have. And I always will."

The next thought formed in his head and the words were out of his mouth before he could second-guess them—the way he'd discounted and second-guessed the worth of *Phrase Fusion*.

"Marry me, Jules. For real."

She pulled back and frowned at him as if he'd suggested they roll in a pile of rotten fish.

"What are you talking about?" she asked.

"I'm talking about us, Jules. You and me. We're good together. We like the same things. We see the world the same way. And we did promise to marry each other if we hit thirty and were both still single."

"No!" She crossed her arms and took a couple of steps backward. "Owen, don't do this. Just don't."

"Why not? Jules, I love you. I have always loved you. It just makes so much sense."

"But you're not *in love* with me, Owen. It's one thing to love someone like a friend, and another to be—" She shook her head as if she were trying to clear away cobwebs or something worse. "No. Just no."

Owen swallowed. Hard. "Are you still hoping things will work out with Ed? Do you still have feelings for him?"

"No. Ed and I were never meant to be anything more than what we were. That ship has sailed. After talking to him today, I have never been more sure of that."

Thank God. There was still a chance for them. "Then marry me, Jules."

Her eyes glimmered with unshed tears. "And what's going to happen when you do fall in love with someone, Owen? I mean *in love*. Romantically. Not like the love you feel for your best friend. Divorce is a hell of a lot harder than a broken fake engagement."

"I could never meet anyone else that I feel this way about." He smiled and took her hands. "Love is funny— the hot, intense *in love* part fades fast. Then you're left with the real thing. That's what we have, Jules. It's what we've always had, but I think we were both too scared we'd ruin it by crossing some imaginary line we'd drawn in the sand."

Still holding her hands, he sobered and dropped down on one knee.

"Juliette, marry me."

Juliette's heartbeat kicked up a notch. This was Owen.

Her best friend, who meant the world to her. He would never hurt her on purpose. So why was he doing this to her? To them?

Completely at a loss for words, she stared at Owen.

She opened her mouth to say something...anything, but she couldn't force a sound to come out.

Really, what was she supposed to say? All she could do was stand there dumbly. She was sure her face was the color of all the blood she could hear rushing and whooshing in her ears. Or maybe the sound was the wind and roar of the sea or something surreal spawned by this weird twist of events.

"Jules?" Owen asked. "Say something. Please?"

She tugged her hand from his and turned away from him. Crossing her arms over her chest, she tried to regain her equilibrium, but the feeling that the bottom had just dropped out of her world—their world—wouldn't go away.

It was a nightmare.

Maybe she was dreaming. The thought gave her temporary hope. She balled her hands into tight fists, feeling the bite of her fingernails as they sank into her palms.

Nope. She was fully awake. So this wasn't one of those bad dreams she'd had too many times before. The ones where she thought Owen was showing true romantic interest in her, only to realize she was the butt of an elaborate joke. Or the recurring dream where Owen came to see her in LA with important news, only to announce that he was marrying someone else. In one dream, he was marrying Kimmy. Another time, it was the actress who was starring in the film she was working on.

But this nightmare was playing out in real time.

She felt Owen's hands on her shoulders, his thumb gently caressing her. He'd done that hundreds of times before and she'd always loved his touch, but right now, it felt dangerous. As if it could hypnotize her and make her give in to this new plan, which he'd laid on the table between them like a delectable feast.

"Look, I know you could do better than me," he said. "But I can guarantee you that no one could care about you more than I do."

She turned around and faced him, despite the war going on in her breaking heart. How long had she day-dreamed of the day her best friend would finally realize he was in love with her and declare that he wanted them to be together?

But he wasn't *in love* with her. That was key. "Hey, buddy, love ya," just wasn't enough.

In her musings, Owen had been *in love* with her. He wasn't proposing marriage because he was high on sealing a business deal or assuaging the guilt of friends throwing them an engagement party or simply wanting to try it on for size.

She'd dreamed of marrying Owen, but not like this. It felt so…weird.

"Can we talk about it?" he asked.

She nodded.

"Come on, let's walk." She let him take her hand, and they started down the beach.

She finally found her voice. "Let's just take a moment and talk about the logistics of the two of us—you and me—actually getting married."

He nodded. "That's fair."

A slow smile spread over his face.

"What?" she asked. "Why are you smiling like that?"

He shrugged. "I just think it would be nice for us to be together. We'd live together. I'd get to wake up with you every morning. Oh…"

His face fell. "I don't expect you to give up your career, Jules. I know you have to be on location when there's a shoot, but could you be based out of Tinsley Cove? That way we could be together when you were between projects."

"You know I'm away for months at a time, Owen. Would you really want to tie yourself down to a wife who was gone more than she was at home? And what about when I'm gone? You'll get lonely. You'll go out and meet people. What if after we get married, you meet the person you're supposed to be with? Then what?"

He didn't answer her.

"Owen. You love me like a sister or like a friend, but you're not *in love* with me. Let's just take a moment and regroup and put everything into perspective. In fact, you know what I want you to do? I want you to think back to the last time you were in love and compare what you think you're feeling for me to what you felt then. Okay?"

He stopped walking and turned to her, but he wasn't saying anything. Juliette thought he was making the mental comparison.

"Tell me," she said. "Who was the last person you were in love with—wait, let me guess. It was your mom's cancer nurse, Kiley, wasn't it?"

He'd always told her about the women he was dating. It wasn't that she remembered him saying he had strong feelings for Kiley as much as that was the first name Juliette could extract from her memory of Owen's long line of girlfriends.

"Nope," he said, staring at his feet.

"Okay, Melissa, then."

"Which one?" he said. "I've gone out with several Melissas."

"I know you have. We're you in love with any of them?"

This time he did look at her. Square in the eyes. "No. I wasn't in love with any of the Melissas. I wasn't in love with the Ashleys or the Emilys or the Taylors. I wasn't in love with any of them because I love you. That's the one true thing I have to tell you. And that will be tomorrow's true thing and the next day's."

She sucked in a quick breath and almost choked on it. She managed to keep her composure, but she felt too fragile to speak.

"I realize it takes two people to make a marriage work," he said. "If you don't love me, I understand. I know this seems like a lot all at once, but..." He shrugged. "If not now, when?"

It was a lot. In fact, it was everything that she had

ever wanted tied up with a virtual red ribbon and hearts. Because she did love him. She'd always loved him, but she also knew that Owen had a history of being all in on things and then suddenly changing his mind.

She thought about all of the careers he'd tried on for size and the revolving door of women he'd dated, the relationships that had seemed promising in the beginning but had always fizzled out for one reason or another.

She crossed her arms and narrowed her eyes at him. "We've been friends since we were toddlers, and you're just now figuring this out? After we've gotten ourselves tangled up in a fake engagement that's getting more complicated by the minute? Interesting timing for you to have this sudden epiphany, Owen."

"It's not a sudden epiphany, Jules. I've known this since—"

She held up her hand. "Just stop, okay?"

"Jules, I'm telling you the truth."

She shook her head.

She could stand by him changing his mind about the jobs and the girlfriends, but she knew she wouldn't recover if she let out all these feelings she'd managed to bottle up all these years—especially the fact that she'd been in love with him since she'd known what love was—and he changed his mind about her…

If that happened, it would be the end of them.

It would have to be the end, because there would be nowhere else for them to go.

There would be no coming back from that—not even friendship.

As she stood there trying to reconcile what was true

and what was…convenient, she realized that maybe she'd rather keep her feelings buried than risk having everything blow up.

If she never told him how she felt, he wouldn't feel pressured and would still be in her life. Things would be neat and tidy and safe.

"Will you please say something?" he said.

Again, she opened her mouth, but no sound came out. So, she shook her head.

"Tell me you don't love me—or couldn't at least grow to love me—and we never have to speak of this again," he added.

She searched his gorgeous face—those sea-green eyes that looked two shades darker right now. That wavy brown hair that always made her fingers itch to touch it. Those lips. Oh, those lips. Since tasting them, she'd started to crave them, and that couldn't be good.

So, no, she couldn't say she didn't love him, because it would be a lie.

Another lie heaped on top of all the others. Lies had gotten them into this mess. She just wanted to stop talking about it. She wanted him to stop pressing her on it because she had buried all of the feelings she'd carried for him deep in her heart. If he kept pressing on that tender spot, she feared it would rip open, everything would spill out and he would realize he'd made a mistake.

"At least you haven't run away screaming," he said. "That's got to be a good sign."

Maybe she should run. Maybe she should turn around and run all the way back to LA and forget about this mess. Except her mother needed her help right now, and really, the weak part of her that had grown weary after holding in all these feelings didn't want to.

In a voice so quiet she almost couldn't hear it, the tiniest ray of hope was pleading, *Stay. Let this play out. See what happens. Because maybe it could work. Maybe Owen really could love you…*

But hope ran back into hiding when an internal bully voice roared, *Are you an idiot? Marry him and I give it six months. If that.*

"I have an idea," Owen said. "I know this probably feels like I'm going from zero to sixty in nothing flat. Let me prove how I feel about you. Let me take you out on dates. I want to treat you like a girlfriend. I mean, we're already engaged. That's what a couple in love should be doing. They should want to spend time together. Will you let me court you, Jules?"

Her mind was spinning.

"If you break my heart, I'll never forgive you, Owen McFadden."

"I will treat your heart like it's made of the finest porcelain."

He pulled her into his arms.

She wanted to say that porcelain was actually quite durable. But then she wondered if maybe it *was* an accurate description of her heart.

She was a resilient woman.

But this resilient woman had never let Owen play with her heart.

Not like this.

Not like he was now… He was kissing her and making her believe that what he was saying just might be true.

She wound her hands into his hair to try and stop herself from freefalling, but she was too far gone.

For a perfect moment, Juliette let go and let herself believe everything the love of her life had said was true—that he had always been *in love* with her, that he was *in love* with her now—but then reality came crashing down.

The truth was, when it came to women, Owen was fickle. For some reason he had bought into their charade with a little too much gusto. Maybe he thought that if they really got married, it would turn their lie into the truth. It certainly would absolve them from disappointing her mom and his family when they announced the breakup.

But what would happen after the shiny newness wore off?

Owen loved women.

No doubt, he would meet the woman he was really meant to be with. They would fall in love, but he would be legally tied to Juliette.

Why was it her lot in life to never be the leading lady? She would always and forever be relegated to the role of best friend.

Once upon a time, she thought that crossing the line with Owen—making love to him—would spell disaster for their friendship. Now she knew that wasn't the end of the line for them, because he meant too much to her. But if she gave in to this moment of weakness and agreed to marry him for real and it didn't work out…

Especially if he met someone else…

She didn't see how they could ever come back from that.

In the name of preserving the one relationship that meant more to her than anything in the world, she had to be the strong one for the both of them.

"No, Owen. Just no."

"I'm not taking no for an answer, Jules. I want you to think about it."

The next day, rather than flying home with Owen, Juliette had rented a car and driven to Los Angeles. He'd asked her if she wanted him to go with her, but she'd told him she needed some time alone.

He hadn't pushed the issue.

Their hosts had been none the wiser, because Owen and Juliette had played their roles until they'd left for the airport, leaving Dan and China Richter waving from their driveway.

Juliette had changed her flight home and taken the rental car after she'd dropped Owen off at the airport. It would've only taken an hour and a half to fly from San Francisco to LAX, but Juliette had opted to make the six-hour drive so she could have time to sort out her life.

Owen had proposed to her.

For real.

She was still trying to wrap her head around it. What had gotten into him?

She hadn't exactly said no. Not a hard no, anyway.

That's why she owed him an answer when she got home to Tinsley Cove.

Why had he muddied the waters?

They'd had a plan, and it had been working fine until Owen had thrown her a curveball.

Actually, they'd had a good, solid friendship that had outlasted any of the romantic relationships they'd gotten themselves tangled up in over the years.

Despite any and all boyfriend troubles, she knew her and Owen's relationship—their friendship—was stronger than anything else.

Why mess with a good thing?

She'd thought he was joking at first, but then she'd realized he'd been serious.

He'd said he wanted to marry because he loved her, not out of romantic love, not because he was *in love* with her, not because he couldn't live without her, but because it made sense.

And that made absolutely zero sense to her.

One of them should've slept on the couch—since neither of them had been strong enough to not get lost in the play that they'd been acting out.

By making love, they had blurred the lines of everything that had once made sense.

Juliette had a feeling that after Owen was back in Tinsley Cove and had a couple of days to think about things, he would come to his senses and realize the two of them getting married would be just about the worst thing they could do.

While she was in California, she had checked in with her mother and Ginny every day. Ginny had confirmed that her mom was doing well. Her mom had told her she didn't need a babysitter anymore. Juliette had laughed and said that that would be the doctor's decision.

When she'd told her that Ingrid and Harry had gotten married and wanted privacy as they started their married life, her mother had been supportive of Juliette driving down to Los Angeles to box up her belongings.

"Is Owen going with you?" she'd asked.

"He offered, but he has some work to do, so I sent him home."

Because her mom had sounded so much better, Juliette had felt better about taking the extra time away to drive to Ingrid's place in LA, where she'd done her best to pretend as if her entire world wasn't imploding.

She was happy for Ingrid and Harry. They were newlyweds and had every right to want the house to themselves as they started their new life together.

Ingrid had told her that she didn't have to move her things out right away. In fact, she'd even offered to take care of packing and getting them to Juliette. But Juliette knew there was nothing like manual labor to help sort out the mind. So she'd spent three days boxing up her things in Ingrid's house and made arrangements to have them shipped to Tinsley Cove.

For now, at least. Since she didn't have a job or a place to live for the next couple of months, it was the only thing that made sense…at least until she figured out what she was going to do with herself.

She'd taken the red-eye from Los Angeles back to the East Coast. After the Uber had dropped off Juliette at her mother's house and she was rolling her suitcases toward the front door, her text tone sounded.

In the split second before she pulled it out of her pocket, her heart quickened with the hope that it was Owen. She hadn't told him when she was coming back to Tinsley Cove—mostly because she hadn't known exactly when she would head back, but also because Owen hadn't asked. In fact, he hadn't called or texted since she'd dropped him off at the airport. It had taken everything she had not to call him because she wanted to hear his voice, she wanted to know that everything between them was going to be okay. But she'd also known that he would ask her if she'd had a chance to think about the proposal.

She had, but the problem was, she hadn't come to a conclusion—all she could think about was that it all felt wrong. Hadn't it been a sign that she hadn't thrown her arms around him and cried an emphatic *yes*?

Maybe the *yes* was in her heart, but it was buried and weighted down under all sorts of suspicions that Owen was doing this for all the wrong reasons. He had a point that the fireworks in relationships did fizzle after a while and then the couple was left with the essence of their relationship.

If it was a strong relationship—even one built on a foundation of friendship—then it would last. If there wasn't a solid base, if the relationship was based purely on lust or physical attraction, it was doomed.

He'd sworn their relationship was built to stand the test of time.

Was it wrong that she wanted to feel that burst of fireworks before she and the man she loved landed in reality?

A little voice inside of her reminded her that she and Owen had certainly experienced something very explosive the night they'd made love. But then, the next night, on the beach, everything had gotten weird. Owen had always been her safe space. He'd always made her laugh. She needed that. She would make darn sure she fixed this.

As she searched for her phone, butterflies shot through her belly, along with a surge of relief that this might be Owen reaching out to her—and if it was Owen, she'd invite him over and cook dinner for him and her mom, then they'd talk things out. They'd fix things together.

As soon as she held her phone in her hand, her hopes were squashed when she saw that the texter wasn't Owen.

It was Ed.

Oh.

She stared at his message in the text bubble.

Ed: Guess where in the world I am.

The buoyancy she'd felt a moment ago when she'd hoped it was Owen was deflated by a sharp stab of annoyance. She was exhausted and didn't want to deal with her ex or the thoughts that were swirling through her mind right now, such as, *Had there ever been fireworks with Ed?*

Sure, there'd been chemistry…but nothing really combustible. Nothing to light her up.

Juliette: I can't even fathom.

She was typing another message telling him that she'd get back to him after she got some sleep. But another text from him came through.

Ed: Turn around. I'm parked on the street right behind you.

What?

She turned around and saw Ed getting out of a rented Ford Explorer.

She hadn't even had a chance to tell her mother or Owen she was home. Her mother was expecting her, but if she was being honest, she was avoiding Owen because they had so much to talk about. He'd press her for answers that she didn't have.

Or he might've come to his senses and realized what a disaster it would be if they really did get married... She wasn't quite ready for them to put Plan Endgame into play.

Now, here was Ed.

Juliette wasn't sure if his sudden appearance complicated matters or gave her a valid reason to push off the dreaded conversation with Owen that she was avoiding.

Time would tell.

She set her bags on the porch and met him halfway down the walk leading to her mother's house.

"Ed, what are you doing here? For that matter, how did you know where to find me?"

"I have my ways," he said, lifting a mischievous eyebrow. "Seriously, I knew you lived in Tinsley Cove because you told me. When you talked about it, you always made it sound so magical."

I did?

"You listed your mom as your emergency contact when we were working on the Van Gogh film. I got it from the files."

Oh. That makes sense.

But why was he here?

A car drove by slowly and then turned right on the next street, which was just two houses down. The sun was shining in Juliette's eyes so she couldn't see in the windows. The person saw her talking to a good-looking guy who was not Owen in front of her mother's house. It was a small town. Rumors tended to catch and stick.

Even so, she was torn over what to do. If she went inside and told her mother she was home from California, it would be difficult to leave Ed standing outside, but she didn't want to invite him in. That would open a can of worms she was not up to dealing with.

Plus, Ed didn't know she was supposedly getting married. Her mother was bound to share the good news, if for no other reason than to make sure Ed understood that Juliette was off the market.

Even though Juliette was fairly certain the Ed ship had sailed and she wasn't on it, she didn't want to draw him into the engagement charade only to have to explain later that things didn't work out.

Casting another glance over her shoulder at the house and ascertaining that her mother probably didn't know she was home, she said, "Let me put my bags in the trunk of your car, and let's go somewhere and talk."

She decided that Springdale Park would be the best place, because sitting on a park bench meant she wouldn't have to introduce Ed to the barista at the Bean and Press coffee shop or the waiter at Harry's on Main.

Once they were situated in an out-of-the-way spot, she said, "So, tell me again, why are you here?"

"Well, I don't think I mentioned the reason earlier."

"Okay, well, now's your chance."

"Actually, I'm multitasking," he said. "In addition to coming to see you, I'm location scouting. I've been watching the reality show *Selling Sandcastle,* and I think Tinsley Cove will make a good location for a movie I've just optioned. If we can get the powers that be with the town to agree to let us film here, it's a done deal. If you have any contacts, maybe you could put in a good word? Of course, if we film here, it would mean a job for you. How about showrunner?"

She did know somebody. Owen's brother Forest was the mayor of Tinsley Cove.

Maybe it was the complicated situation—the fact that she and Owen were supposed to break up after she went back to California—but she wasn't enthusiastic about working on a movie in her hometown. Having had a break and no longer having an affordable place to live in Los Angeles, she wasn't sure if she wanted to rejoin the grind.

If she was being honest with herself, she was tired of the uncertainty and the competitiveness.

She was tired of doing her damnedest, working long hours without days off and always being there when they needed her, only to be overlooked because the unexperienced niece of someone higher on the food chain wanted the job for which she'd busted her butt.

It felt as if she were standing at a fork in the road.

A four-pronged fork in the road, actually. If that made any sense. Two prongs were work. The other two prongs were Owen—and she couldn't even think about which direction to go with that one.

But whether or not she wanted a career change felt more certain.

She did want a change.

Granted, she didn't know what she wanted to do next, but she knew she no longer wanted to work in a field that was so unpredictable.

Ed must've read the uncertainty on her face. "Whether or not we end up shooting here, I miss you, Juliette. We were good together."

Were they?

Now that she'd put a little distance between Ed and herself, she could see the pattern more clearly. Ed was all hers if they were working on a project together. However, if it was more advantageous for him to hire someone else, she was out.

"Why didn't you fight for me for *Argentine Tango*, Ed?"

A hiccup of a laugh preceded his answer. "You know how Hazel Shine is. When she's attached to the picture, what Hazel wants, Hazel gets. Her niece wanted the job. It was a stipulation of Hazel doing the film."

Of course, and she was so damned tired of being the understanding one whom no one fought for.

She'd heard that Ed and Hazel's niece had been attached at the hip during the production. She had friends in the industry. People talked. She thought about asking him if he'd considered changing the name of the position from production assistant to Ed's Sidepiece. But that would only make her sound bitter. She wasn't. She'd gone into the relationship with Ed of her own volition. He had not coerced or pressured her.

The truth was, she was tired of the whole phony game, and maybe she was making Ed her scapegoat, her reason why she wanted out.

But it wasn't his fault.

Dammit, she was tired of being attracted to men who couldn't commit.

For once in her life, she wanted to be the one who got the star treatment.

Even if it meant she had to be alone for a while— maybe even work in a movie theater to make enough money to get by.

Once upon a time, she'd left Tinsley Cove for Los Angeles to find herself and work in the movies. She'd always loved movies. They had been her escape growing up—especially after her dad died. Now, it seemed like she had come full circle.

She would tell Ed no; that was a no-brainer.

She loved Owen. That was another no-brainer. She just needed to figure out how to save their relationship.

The path forward wasn't clear. That scared her more than anything. Somehow, they needed to find a way back.

Chapter Eleven

When the knock sounded on Owen's front door, he thought it might be Juliette coming over to talk about everything. He wasn't even sure she was home yet, but the last person he expected to see at his door was Kimmy Ogilvie.

"Oh, hey," he said, even though he didn't want to talk to Kimmy right now. "What's up?"

He wanted to talk to Jules. They needed to talk about them. He needed to know if she'd made up her mind about whether or not she would marry him. Because surely she'd had enough time to process everything and see that getting married was the only thing that made sense.

He loved her, and if she didn't believe that, he was going to find a way to prove it to her.

At the very least, he wanted to pull her into his arms and kiss her, but the moment when it could've been spontaneous had passed. Or maybe that was his problem. Maybe he was treading so lightly that he was sending mixed signals.

He hadn't been able to eat or sleep since he'd been home.

A mental replay of the proposal kept playing in his

head on a loop—the moment the words had fallen out of his mouth and he'd found himself on one knee.

Each time it replayed in his mind and he relived it, he felt more and more certain that it had been the right thing to do. If he could go back he wouldn't change it. Except for her response. In that do-over, Jules would say yes.

He finally understood why none of his other relationships had worked. He loved Jules.

He didn't understand this *in love*/I love you quandary she was having. He thought that he might see it if he had time to step back and think about it.

He loved her. Period.

If she wanted him to say, Jules, I'm *in love* with you, he would. On the beach, he hadn't wanted her to think he was patronizing her. That's why he hadn't said it.

Now he knew words were words. Feelings were feelings.

He loved and was *in love* with her.

They'd left things up in the air the other night because he'd wanted her to be true to her heart. That's why he was willing to wait and to win her over, if necessary.

But that wasn't going to happen until he had a chance to see her and talk to her.

"Um, can I come in?" Kimmy had an edge to her voice.

"Sure." He stepped back and motioned her inside.

She stood in the foyer, not shy about looking around and taking in the place. It was the first time she'd been over.

"So, not to be rude, but why are you here?" he asked.

"I suppose I should've called first, but I decided it was best if I came over because what I have to say, I need to tell you in person, Owen."

The colorful dress she wore hung on her shapelessly and emphasized the boniness of her collarbones and shoulders.

Not that he was looking at her shape and sizing her up, but she looked even thinner than when Owen had last seen her at the wedding. It was almost alarming.

He thought about asking her if she was okay, but Kimmy started talking first.

"Owen, let's sit down."

She didn't wait for him. She walked into his living room and made herself at home on the sofa—the same sofa where things had started between him and Jules before they'd left for Cali.

Kimmy perched on the edge of the cushion and crossed one sandal-clad foot over the other.

Owen sat in the chair across from her.

"Look, I'm just going to cut to the chase," she said. "Did you and Juliette break up?"

"What? No. Why?"

What had she heard? What news did she have that made her feel like she needed to come over and break it in person? For that matter, how could she have heard anything?

"Well, I'm sorry to be the bearer of bad news, but I just saw Juliette and her ex-boyfriend, Ed, in town at Springdale Park, and they looked pretty cozy."

Kimmy's mouth turned down at the corners. She was

trying to look sad for him, but Owen caught the hint of victory that glimmered in her eyes.

Jules had just seen him in California. Why was he here?

Had he come all this way to try to win her back?

Something green and thorny and wholly unpleasant sprouted in Owen's gut and wound itself around his insides.

Of course, she was within her right to see Ed if that's what she wanted, but it would've been nice if she had warned him.

She hadn't even told him she was back in town.

Nice.

Well, this put a wrinkle in things. He shouldn't jump to conclusions.

"You said they were getting cozy. What exactly do you mean by that?"

As soon as the words left his mouth, he regretted them. He sounded jealous.

He *was* jealous.

But Kimmy was the last person he wanted to arm with such personal information. Letting his jealousy show might have been marginally better than pretending he didn't care that his *fiancée* was in the park canoodling with her ex. But he needed to get control over this situation, or Kimmy would.

"Jules and Ed have worked together in the past, and Jules is looking for another movie." He shrugged, hoping to look nonchalant.

"Well…um, I also know they dated, but it's good that he's in town then." She shifted on the sofa, switching out the foot that had been wrapped around her ankle with the other one. "Exes can still be friends. But Owen, marriage is a huge step."

"I know it is," he said, wondering how she knew Jules and Ed had dated.

"Believe me, I've been thinking about it ever since Richard proposed." She fidgeted with her engagement ring, twisting it around on her finger. "Especially since seeing you again."

Okay, here we go.

"Is that why you're here, Kimberly?"

"I'm here because I don't want you to make a mistake."

"Well, I appreciate that, but it's been more than a decade since you and I have seen each other, and I've managed not to ruin my life."

"Have you?" she asked.

"Excuse me?"

"I didn't mean it that way," she said. "I just—I guess, ever since I ran into Juliette at the Primrose boutique, I've had a weird feeling that something was off. And this afternoon, when I was out for my walk and I saw her sitting there with her ex-boyfriend—"

"How did you know the guy she was with was her ex?" Owen asked.

For that matter, it might not even be Ed. Could Kimmy have mistaken another woman for Jules? Again, he had to circle back to this question: if Jules was back from California, wouldn't she have let him know?

"Google." Kimmy flipped up the palm of her right hand as if implying, *Duh*.

"Why would you google Jules?"

She squinted at him as if he were an idiot. "Because she has this awesome life working in the movies, and I wanted to know more. What's wrong with that?"

He shrugged, knowing better than to say what he was thinking to Kimmy. It would lead to multiple rounds of one-upping until he acquiesced and she was satisfied that she'd won.

"It's not stalkerish at all, if that's what you were thinking," she said.

Yep. That about sums it up. I didn't say it, but you did.

"Owen. Please listen to me. I'm afraid she's going to hurt you. She's sitting in the park with her ex in front of God and all of Tinsley Cove. That can't be good."

"Think about it," he said. "You and I dated once and we're alone in my house now. Nothing untoward is happening. And people are not going to jump to the wrong conclusions. At least Jules and Ed are out in the open, in front of God and all of Tinsley Cove, as you put it. Thanks for your concern, Kimmy, but I'm fine. You don't need to worry about me."

"But that's the thing, Owen, I do worry about you. In fact, since I saw you at the cocktail party, I haven't been able to stop thinking about you."

Oh no.

The hair on the back of his neck stood up. He braced himself because he had an uncomfortable inkling about where this conversation was heading.

"I've been thinking about you and me, Owen. Did you ever wonder if we're both about to make a big mistake by marrying other people? Now that we've had a chance to get out in the world, maybe we need to re-visit what we had."

The room felt claustrophobic. He stood.

"Kimberly, you and I dated when we were in high school. We are completely different people now. You are probably just having cold feet. Once you're married, you'll realize Richard is the only man for you and you did the right thing by accepting his proposal."

She stood up, too.

"That's the thing, Owen. There is no Richard. I made up the whole thing because I'm thirty-one years old. Almost everyone else we went to school with is getting married. I thought that if I attended the wedding with-out my fiancé—" she put air quotes around the word *fiancé* "—you would realize in the nick of time that you still had feelings for me and we'd end up getting back together."

Owen backed toward the door.

"That's the thing about me, Kimberly. I don't make a habit of moving in on other men's fiancées. So, you don't know me as well as you think you do. That will happen when you haven't seen someone for more than a decade."

"The thing is, Owen, I have been keeping tabs on you. Especially since you've been on *Selling Sandcastle*. I haven't missed an episode. So, I do know you. You're still the same old you, and I'm still the same old me."

Apparently so.

"We owe it to ourselves to explore these feelings," she said.

Owen's mind raced. He didn't want to be cruel to her, but he needed to make her understand that it had been a long time since he'd had feelings for her. Even then, he'd been a hormone-driven teenager.

"Kimberly, I don't want to hurt your feelings, but I love Jules. I'm marrying her."

Kimberly made a *pffft* sound and waved away his words like they smelled bad.

"It's Juliette, Owen." She made a face that started his blood simmering. "How could you be in love with *her*?"

"I've been in love with her for a long time. She's my soulmate."

Kimberly snorted and rolled her eyes. "Well, judging by the looks of things in the park, she might be making other plans."

Owen opened the front door, the unspoken invitation for her to leave.

Kimmy raised her chin and pursed her lips before saying, "I'll be here for you after things fall apart."

"Thanks, but things between Jules and me aren't going to fall apart." *I'll make sure of it.*

"Yeah, well, you might want to hurry," Kimberly said. "I saw her putting suitcases in the trunk of his car."

"Suitcases? I thought you saw them in the park?"

"I was driving by her mom's house and saw Ed putting suitcases in his trunk."

So they might not belong to Jules.

But it was still strange.

"A moment ago, you said you were out for a walk—"

"Okay, so I was driving by her house." She made a face a shrugged as if he was splitting hairs.

The woman couldn't keep her story straight.

"When she got into his car, I was curious so I followed them to the park."

He wanted to ask for details. *What was their body language?*

Did he hold her hand?

Did they kiss?

No.

He wouldn't let Kimberly know those things concerned him.

He would get the story straight from Jules. If she was in love with Ed, he would learn how to live with that. But he couldn't give up without trying to make her see that he loved her.

That they were the real deal.

As Kimberly started to walk away, she turned back to Owen.

"Owen, all I ever wanted was a man that looked at me the way you look at Juliette." She bit down on her bottom lip. He wished he knew what to say to make her feel better, but he didn't have the words.

"What I said about pretending to be engaged… Will you promise me you won't tell anyone? It's humiliating."

He smiled at her. "Pretend engagement? I have no idea what you're talking about."

"Owen McFadden, you're a good man. Juliette is lucky that you love her."

Owen closed the front door. Again, he thought about how he had proposed to Jules in California, how Jules had said she didn't believe that Owen was in love with her. Since they'd been apart, he'd been racking his brain for a way to show her.

Now he knew exactly what he needed to do.

Juliette had gotten home from talking to Ed just in time to take her mother to the doctor. Helen had gotten the all clear from her doctor. The pacemaker was doing its job, and Helen's body had accepted the device well. It had been welcome news.

Selfishly, the distraction of the appointment had been a good thing for Juliette because it had temporarily taken her mind off of the chaos that had started swirling since she and Owen had gone to California.

Now that she was home, even though she tried to focus on the good—her mother was feeling well and acting more like herself again—the angst that Juliette had tried to shove into the recesses of her mind was now crawling out to the forefront.

She had so many things to sort out before she could figure out her way forward. From this angle, it seemed like an insurmountable mountain.

For now, she had to put it all aside and concentrate on getting lunch for her mother and herself sorted.

Helen followed Juliette into the kitchen and said, "Honey, you have basically put your life on hold to look after me, and I hope you do know how much I appreciate all you've done for me. How lucky am I to have such a wonderful, selfless daughter like you, Juliette." Helen folded her daughter into a hug, and there was something about her mother's tender touch and the gratitude she expressed that nearly brought down the dam that Juliette had erected around her emotions.

She was bone-tired and emotionally spent. She was tired of carrying around the burden of lies and keeping up the display that went along with this show. She needed to pull herself together and get through lunch, then she could take a shower and sleep.

Everything always made more sense after a shower and a nap.

Until then, to regain her equilibrium, she turned away from her mother and started foraging through the kitchen cabinets for cans of soup.

Few foods were more comforting than tomato soup and grilled cheese. The makings were staples in her mom's kitchen, and the meal was easy to put together.

"Well, I hope you don't mind putting up with me a little bit longer since I'm essentially homeless right now," she said as she gathered the ingredients. "Don't worry. I'll get a job here so I can help with the expenses."

Helen, who was now seated at the kitchen table, clapped her hands like a gleeful child. "I am delighted. Of course, I understand it will only be until after you and Owen get married, but I do have to confess when you first told me that you were moving out of Ingrid's place, I was afraid that you'd want to move in directly with Owen. So, I couldn't be happier that you want to stay with me for the last few months of your single life."

Juliette felt her emotions slipping again. She and Owen needed to come up with another plan. The breakup wouldn't be as seamless as they had planned since she was staying in Tinsley Cove rather than going back to California.

Even so, it wasn't fair to keep up the ruse. Her mother was well again, and Owen had nailed down the financing he needed. They needed to get back to reality.

"Speaking of the wedding," Helen said.

They hadn't been—not directly. As Juliette flipped the grilled cheese sandwiches, she bit down on her lower lip to keep from revealing too much to her mother.

"I wanted to talk to you about something," Helen said.

Juliette turned around and set the plated sandwiches on the table. The happiness her mother had exuded earlier was replaced with something that seemed like nervousness.

"Is everything okay?"

The doctor had given her a good report. Juliette had heard it with her own ears.

"What is it, Mom? Is everything okay?"

"Don't be alarmed, honey. I'm fine. It's just that Bunny called me yesterday and asked me to try and convince you to participate in a scene with the three of us at Primrose Bridal. That producer fellow, Dalton, wants to film you trying on wedding dresses. Bunny and I would be there as your support system. He will pay you. Handsomely, judging by what Bunny said, because he really wants you and Owen and your happy ending to be a part of the show's final episode. I'm thinking that since he wants the show to end with each person in the McFadden family getting their happy ending, as Bunny put it, that's why he's willing to offer you a goodly amount."

Wedding dresses?

He wanted to film her trying on wedding dresses for her pretend mother-in-law and all the world to see?

"No. I can't."

"Honey, think about it. If you do this, and it shouldn't be hard—you'll be trying on wedding gowns soon enough anyway, and if you're worried about it being bad luck for Dalton and them to film you in the one you want to wear for the wedding, just don't try on *the dress*."

Juliette was shaking her head, and she felt tears breeching the dam, but her mother was looking at her soup bowl as she talked and didn't notice.

"But if you do this, you'll probably make enough money so that you won't need a part-time job between now and the wedding. This opportunity is a godsend."

Helen put her hand over Juliette's shaking hand, then looked up in surprise. "Honey, you're crying. What's wrong?"

She couldn't lie to her mother any longer, but she owed it to Owen to talk to him before she came clean to anyone.

"You don't have to film for that show, if that's what's upsetting you," Helen said. "In fact, Dalton said, as a fallback plan, that he could film Bunny and me looking at mother-of-the-bride-and-groom dresses. We can do that if you'd rather."

She was squeezing Juliette's hand earnestly now, but Juliette couldn't form words that would move through her sobs. Plus, if she said anything else, it would just add to the Jenga tower of lies that they'd built that was precariously close to collapsing.

She and Owen needed to sort this out before she said anything to anyone else.

Even her mother.

As if reading her mind, Helen asked, "Is everything okay between you and Owen?"

Juliette just sat there sobbing.

What was she supposed to say? Things had never been worse? She was about to lose the best friend she'd ever had…the only man she'd ever really loved? But if she said that, she'd have to go back to the beginning and tell her mother that the romance and the engagement had all been a lie.

Her mom would never understand that he had proposed for real, but she couldn't marry him because he didn't love the way he should if he was proposing marriage. Marriage was *until death do us part*. Not *'til the right love comes along*. That could only lead to heartbreak and the end of any relationship they might be able to salvage if they called off this farce now.

"I'm just exhausted," Juliette said. "I need to talk to Owen about a few things."

After she excused herself and headed toward her room, she realized that the only thing in this whole web of lies that had been real was that she really did love Owen.

It was too bad that he didn't love her the same way.

Chapter Twelve

Owen could tell Juliette had been crying when she called to say that they needed to talk as soon as possible. It wasn't the time to question her, to ask why she hadn't called to let him know she was home.

Why had she been sitting in the park with her ex-boyfriend?

Was he still her ex?

All he'd said was that he would pick her up in ten minutes. She'd sounded relieved when she'd said she would walk to the park that was down the street from her mother's house and wait for him. They could go somewhere from there.

It made sense that she didn't want to have it out—if that's what they were going to do…because he wasn't going to give her up without a fight—in public. It might take a minute to settle things, and he could understand why she wouldn't want to do it at the park down the street from her mother's house.

Judging by the sound of her voice, Owen had a sinking feeling that she didn't have good news for him. Even so, he knew where he was going to take her. He couldn't believe she'd been home all this time and they hadn't gone there before now.

As he pulled up to the curb that ran alongside the park, he saw her sitting on one of the swings. She was the only person there, which surprised him since every time he'd driven by the place, which was in the middle of a residential neighborhood, it had always been populated by young mothers and their children and nannies with their charges.

He'd never really thought about having kids before, but the random thought of what it would be like if he and Jules brought their children there popped into his head, and he didn't hate it.

But they had a lot of territory to cover before they could cross that bridge.

He got out of the car and saw that she was already walking toward him.

He'd guessed right. Her red eyes and tearstained face proved that she'd been crying.

Even though he was dying inside over the possibility of what she might have in store for him, he smiled and took a chance by holding out his arms.

He held his breath for a moment, but soon enough, she was in his arms hugging him back. However, it didn't take her long to step back and cross her arms as she reclaimed her personal space.

He could give her that much. Clearly, she had things on her mind. They had some pretty weighty things to discuss. He gently ushered her to the car, and they both got in.

"Where should we go?" she asked as she buckled her seat belt.

"I know the perfect place," he said.

"Of course you do." She flashed him a sad smile, but at least she was sounding a little more like herself.

He drove along the highway that bordered the coast for a few miles. They rode in silence.

Finally, he asked, "When did you get in?"

"This morning. I took the red-eye, which is why I look like this. I was going to call you."

"You did call me."

"I know. I meant I wanted to call you earlier, but I went to the doctor with my mom, and when we got back, I made lunch for her."

"Is your mom okay?"

"She is. She got a great report from the doctor. So that's good."

And what about you and Ed?

He wasn't going to say that out loud.

However, in that uncanny way she had of reading his mind, she said, "And I might as well tell you that Ed is in town because I'm sure someone else will, eventually. He showed up at the house before I could even take my bags inside. We went to Springdale Park and talked about a few things."

Owen had so many questions. He didn't even know where to start.

"I know," he said. "Good news travels fast in a place like Tinsley Cove."

"Who told you?"

"Do you really want to know?"

She didn't answer as he steered the car off the road.

"Oh my gosh," she said. "This is Secret Spot."

Secret Spot, as they called it, was a niche that was

tucked away from the beach behind a rock formation. The two of them used to hang out there on occasion. It was their safe spot. More than that, it was *their* spot. They'd never shared it with anyone. No one else in their friend group had ever found it because it was about ten miles farther down the beach from where everyone used to hang out.

They got out of the car and walked to the spot.

Judging by the broken beer bottles and other debris, they weren't the only ones who had discovered it. Today, though, it was free of people, and that was all that mattered right now.

Despite the emotional barometer, it was a nice day. Mostly sunny with a few clouds, and the temperature was mild as long as the sun wasn't beating down. Owen wished he would've suggested that they bring their bathing suits. But he hadn't realized that they were going to end up here until he'd seen Jules sitting alone at the park.

"Owen, I haven't thought about this place in years."

Because it felt less awkward to do something rather than sit there and look at her, waiting for one of them to start talking, he began picking up the broken bottle pieces and depositing them into a pile. He had a plastic bag in the trunk of his car. He'd put it in a garbage can before they left.

"Same. Lots of memories, huh?"

"Yeah, but it looks like others have discovered it. I can't believe none of our friends did when we were in school." Their gazes caught, and she pulled her face into a frown. "Be careful, and don't cut yourself."

"I'll be fine," he said, resuming his task. Because if he stayed busy, she wouldn't notice that his hands were shaking.

"I hope so," she said.

He stopped and looked at her.

"We'll get through this," he said.

"Will we?"

He nodded and picked up another piece of glass. "As far as I'm concerned, we will."

He was about to tell her that, as far as he was concerned, the proposal still stood. He loved her and—but a shard of brown glass that had been hidden under a tangle of washed-up seaweed gouged his thumb.

He bit off an expletive. "Sorry about that. I cut myself."

"Oh no, Owen. I'm sorry. Let me see."

He held out his hand. "No, it's fine."

Trying to staunch the bleeding, he wrapped it in the tail of his black shirt.

"You need to clean it," she said. "I have some disinfecting wipes and hand sanitizer in my purse. That should help until we can get you some antibiotic ointment and a bandage. Do you think you need stitches?"

"No. I'm fine. It's just a cut."

She took his hand in hers and examined it.

His heartbeat quickened. All he could feel was the warmth of her skin touching his. All he wanted was to make her understand that he did love her—that he was *in love* with her. He'd never felt this way about anyone else, and if she would just give him a chance, he would prove it.

She made a tourniquet out of a sterilizing wipe by tying it around his thumb. When she squirted the hand sanitizer on it, she said, "I'm sorry. I know that must hurt."

He shook his head. "I didn't feel anything."

Their gazes snared. "Except how much I love you," he said.

"Owen..." She took a step back.

"No, Juliette, will you just hear me out? Please?"

She looked at him for a few beats, and he was stricken by the sadness in her eyes. Finally, she gave a single nod and crossed her arms over her pink blouse as if they were a shield to protect her from his words.

The ocean roared in the distance, and the wind seemed to pick up as the sun went behind a cloud.

"That night that you brought me home after the graduation party," he said. "That night that I kissed you and said what I said. I meant it. I meant it then and I mean it now. Honestly, I think the possibility that we would both end up together one day kept me from falling for anyone else. Because I loved you, Jules. I was in love with you then, and I'm in love with you now. It's always been you, Jules."

She shook her head. "Then why didn't you tell me that sooner?"

"I don't know. I guess it has always been just one of those things that I've lived with—"

She made a face, and he realized that he was starting to make a mess of things.

"No, what I mean is, your heart beats every day, but you don't consciously think about it living in your chest and you carrying it around with you everywhere you go."

Okay, he was just digging himself in deeper.

"Ugh," he growled. "Maybe this is why I never told you, because look at how I'm making a mess of things? I've never been very good with words. I'm a tech geek. You know that."

That brought a whisper of a smile to her lips, but it faded just as quickly as it had appeared.

"What I haven't told you is that after we kissed after the graduation party, I came over to your house the next morning to talk to you, but you were already gone."

She narrowed her eyes at him. "What did you want to talk to me about?"

"About this." He gestured back and forth between them. "About the feelings I had—and continue to have—for you."

"Okay, but you've had thirteen years to tell me. Why now?"

"Maybe we should talk about *why not* then," he said. "We went to different schools. You ended up working on the opposite side of the country. If I'd told you then, what do you think would've happened? It might have ruined everything. I didn't want you to give up your dream. It's taken me a while to figure out what my purpose in this world is. I couldn't exactly have come to California and swept you off your feet. I had nothing to offer you except for my charm and my excruciatingly bad way with words."

This time her face softened and she laughed, but she still didn't say anything.

"I actually wrote you a letter," he said. "I was bringing it to you when I came over that morning that you left for college. It explains everything."

He took it out of his back pocket and held up his hands. Her mouth dropped open, and then she abruptly shut it. "I know—why didn't I send it to you? For all the reasons I said a moment ago. Because after you left, and I got home and had a chance to think it through, I knew it wasn't fair to you. I had nothing to offer you but my love. Now, I have that love that's been compounding daily, plus I have a viable business."

Her eyes widened. "Are things signed and sealed with Dan?"

"I signed the papers and mailed them off this morning."

She gasped and threw her arms around him, but then stepped back.

"I'm so happy for you, Owen. But I guess that means we really don't need to pretend anymore, do we?"

"No, we don't need to pretend."

He handed the letter to her. "I want you to take this home and read it. After you've had time to think about it, let's talk again. Then if you want to call off the engagement, I'll understand."

Back in her bedroom, Juliette smoothed her hand over the white envelope that Owen had given her. It was yellowed across the top edge and had a crease across the center where he'd folded it in half and put it in his back pocket. Her name was scrawled in faded blue script across the front.

Owen's handwriting.

She traced it with her finger.

The envelope had that flattened look of a missive that had been left to languish in a stack of forgotten mementos.

Owen had said he'd found it in the box his mother had given him that day at the Sandcastle Real Estate office when they'd told his parents they were engaged.

The memory tightened the knot that had been ever present in her stomach since they'd agreed to this ruse. Now it had served its purpose. They'd both gotten what they wanted—her mother was well and could handle the truth. Owen was well on his way to making his dream a reality.

Even though he'd won over his investor, Owen hadn't looked as happy as she thought he would. He'd looked worried when he'd handed the envelope to her. If not romantic, his nerves had been endearing. Her visceral reaction had been to hug him and tell him everything would be okay.

But would it be fine?

Would they be okay?

Maybe they would since Owen seemed resigned to accept her answer after she read the letter, but honestly, she didn't know.

Juliette turned the envelope over in her hand. She ran a finger over the area where the envelope was sealed, where he had licked it with his mouth—the mouth that had covered hers so passionately…that had explored her body—

She needed to stop torturing herself like this.

Just read it and deal with it.

She opened the envelope, then pulled out and unfolded the letter.

June 2, 2006
Dear Jules,
Here we are, wrapping up one of the most important chapters of our lives. Can you believe it? Not so long ago, this day seemed so far away—like it would never get here. I think you wanted this time to come more than I did because you've always known what you wanted.

Me, on the other hand, not so much. Until now.

I don't know why it took that long for me to realize it.

Promise me you won't freak out after you read this, but before you go, I have to tell you, I'm in love with you. I know my timing isn't great, but to be honest with you, I guess I didn't fully realize what these feelings for you really meant.

Everything changed last night when we kissed—for me, at least.

I'm in love with you, Jules.

Maybe I'm an idiot, but I think it took the reality that we will be away from each other for me to realize that I've always been in love with you.

I hope you feel the same way. After you get this letter, if you feel the same way, call me and let's figure out when I can come see you and we can talk about it.

You probably thought it was the beer talking

last night when I said if we weren't married when we were thirty that we should marry each other. I absolutely meant it, except for one little change. If you feel the same way, let's not wait until we're thirty. No, I'm not proposing. Not yet. We need to experience life a little bit before we take that step. But I do hope you'll wait for me, Jules.

Please know I'm not trying to stop you from going after your dream. You've always loved the movies. You've been accepted into film school, and it's important for you to go after your dreams. I'm still trying to figure out what I want to do with myself, but that doesn't have to keep us apart—at least not forever.

I love you, Jules. Always have. Always will.
Owen

By the time Juliette got to the bottom of the letter, tears were flowing down her face.

She felt as if all the air had been knocked out of her and new life had been breathed into her. She wanted to run to him and throw her arms around him and tell him that she loved him. Always had, always would. But one thing nagged at her, and she had to ask Owen in person. She needed him to look her in the eyes when he answered.

She grabbed her purse and the letter and went flying out of her room.

"Juliette?" her mother said when she nearly ran into her in the hallway. "Good heavens, honey, you're crying again. What's wrong?"

"I'm just…in love."

Her mother's brow wrinkled.

"I'll tell you more later, but right now, I need to go and see Owen."

When she yanked open the front door, Owen was standing on the front porch.

"You read the letter?" he asked.

Juliette swiped at tears and held up the paper. "Yeah."

They both started to talk at the same time. They stopped, but then talked over each other again.

Finally, Owen held up his hand. "You first."

"I just have one question," she said. "Why did you not send me this letter after you wrote it? Better yet, why did you wait all these years to tell me this?"

Owen took in a deep breath and rubbed the back of his neck.

"Let's sit down." He gestured to the porch steps.

After they were settled next to each other on the top step, he said, "Like I told you, I came over the next morning, but you were already gone."

"Yes, Mom and I decided to leave early because we wanted to make a couple of stops along the way. The car was already packed, and I felt like we'd already said our goodbyes."

Owen groaned and scrubbed his face with his palm. "Yeah, well, that kiss and the let's-get-married-when-we're-thirty proposal made me realize that I loved you. I didn't want you to go away without knowing. I wrote it all in the letter."

"Except for what changed your mind…why you never sent it."

Owen stared at his hands, then looked Juliette in the eyes.

"I was going to mail it, but I didn't have your address at school. Remember, you called a few days after you got to school and I asked you for it."

"I do remember that."

"You sounded so happy, Jules. You were having so much fun. You even told me about a guy you'd met who'd asked you out."

"I don't remember that."

"Well, you did. You also said you felt like your life was finally changing. You were no longer pigeonholed as the resident nerd like everyone back in Tinsley Cove thought of you. You said, 'Who knew I just had to leave town to start over?'"

She nodded. "It was kind of freeing."

"I know. I could hear it in your voice. I started thinking about things, started assessing what I had to offer you. I mean, I was going to college locally, and you seemed like you had this big adventure ahead of you. My feelings for you didn't change, and it's probably because of how much I loved you that I couldn't saddle you with all that. Just because I'd finally sorted out my feelings for you didn't mean you wanted to be bogged down by them. You were—you still are—my best friend, and I'd rather have you in my life as a friend than to lose you over a one-sided love ultimatum."

The tears were falling, and Juliette was shaking her head.

"It's fine," he said, taking her hand. "We can call off

the engagement. I love you too much to force you into anything you don't want. No hard feelings."

She pressed the index finger of her free hand to his lips.

"It's not one-sided," she said. "It took getting engaged to you to realize that I've been in love with you my entire life, too. What are we going to do about it?"

"Give me the ring," he said.

He didn't wait for her to do it. He picked up her hand and slid it off her finger, smiling at her puzzled expression.

"Come here," he said.

She followed him where he led her, up the steps and onto the porch. Out of the corner of her eye, Juliette saw the living room curtain move.

Her mother was watching, no doubt. She'd figure out a way to explain…once she understood what was happening.

Owen kneeled down and took her hand. "Maybe the fourth time will be the charm. Juliette Margaret Kingsbury, will you marry me?"

"Of course I will," she said through streaming tears. "Owen, I love you."

He pulled her into his arms and covered her mouth with his.

A moment later, the front door opened. "Is everything okay out here?" Helen's anxious gaze darted back and forth between them. "Juliette, honey, why are you crying?"

"I'm crying because I love him. And he loves me."

Helen nodded, but her expression belied her pretending to understand. "But, Owen, you already proposed to her. It looked like you were proposing again."

Owen and Juliette looked at each other and exchanged a secret smile.

"I was renewing my proposal because I wanted to make sure Jules understood exactly how important she is to me. Once she's my wife, my life will be complete."

Helen's hand fluttered to her throat. "Oh my. That's so romantic. It's just like in that movie when Tom Cruise tells that Zellweger woman that she completes him." She fanned her face as if she were fending off her own happy tears. "Well, I'll leave you two lovebirds alone."

"To rephrase the words of that *Zellweger woman*, Owen McFadden, you had me at proposal number four. Or was it number three?"

"That depends," he said. "There was the one in the hospital cafeteria."

"Yes, that one was particularly romantic."

He laughed. "Number two was when I put the ring on your finger. Number three was on the beach in California and number four…"

"Actually, you had me at first sight…all those years ago."

In the middle of Primrose Bridal, Helen held up a princess-style dress with so much skirt that, even on the hanger, it eclipsed Juliette's petite mom. "What about this one, Juliette?"

"That's a lot of dress, Mom," Juliette said.

"Perfect! I'll set it aside so Claudia can put it in the fitting room," Helen said.

"Oh, look at this one." Bunny held up a slim-cut, strapless, figure-hugging gown, which wasn't Juliette's style, either.

"That one isn't quite enough dress," she said.

"Good, add that one to the try-on pile, too," Bunny said.

Juliette had agreed to film a scene for the final season of *Selling Sandcastle* with the stipulation that she wouldn't try on any dresses that she might actually wear in November, when she and Owen were getting married. It was so much more fun going through the dresses when she really was engaged to the man she loved. Her best friend.

She and Owen had decided not to tell anyone about the path that had led them to true love. Because all married couples had their secrets, and as long as the secrets belonged to the two of them, it didn't matter what anyone else thought.

Juliette had just stepped out of the fitting room in the princess gown with the voluminous skirt when the bells over the bridal shop door sounded and in walked Kimberly Ogilvie, dressed to the nines in an expensive-looking pair of black pants and a black silk top underneath her Burberry trench coat. Her platinum-blond hair was perfectly coiffed.

Déjà vu, Juliette thought as she stepped onto the dais, which was surrounded by three mirrors.

Kimberly gasped. "You look beautiful, Juliette. You truly do."

Kimberly seemed different today. No traces of mean-girl Kimmy. Today, she seemed humbler.

"What can I help you with, Kimberly?" asked Claudia, the shop owner.

"Nothing, but thanks. I saw Juliette through the shop window, and I wanted to come in to tell her she looked gorgeous."

Well...wow. Okay.

But something was brewing. Juliette could feel it in her bones.

"I hope this dress is a contender," Kimmy said. "You really do look like a princess."

It wasn't, of course, but Juliette smiled and said, "Thanks, Kimberly. It's nice of you to say that."

"Actually, I'm here for a reason," Kimberly said. "I have a confession to make."

She pursed her candy-apple-red lips together as if she were weighing her words, further adding to the odd behavior.

"I'll just come out with it," she said. "At first, I didn't believe that you and Owen were really engaged. I ran into Patty Jones, who told me she'd seen you and Owen when your mother was in the hospital. She told me that Helen had been confused and thought Owen was her son-in-law-to-be."

"Oh, I was so out of it, honey. I thought butterflies were carrying me around the hospital. No one should've paid any attention to me," said Helen.

Kimmy gave Helen a quick, practiced smile, then turned back to Juliette. "Well, Patty told me that you said you and Owen weren't engaged." Slipping back into her Kimmy persona for a moment, she narrowed her eyes at Juliette, who braced herself for an onslaught of accusations from her former nemesis.

Only, this time, Kimmy could poke and prod all she wanted. Juliette and Owen really were engaged. Juliette's left thumb found the band of her engagement ring on her ring finger. It was like a touchstone that brought her peace every time she felt it there.

"Then I realized that I was just projecting my own guilty conscience onto you," Kimberly said.

"What do you mean?" Juliette asked.

"Did Owen not tell you?"

Juliette must've looked confused because Kimberly said, "No? Well, I might as well come clean to you, too. I'm not engaged."

"I'm so sorry, Kimberly. I didn't know that you and Richard had broken up."

"There was no Richard and no engagement. I made it up because I was embarrassed to come back to Tinsley Cove still single when everyone was getting married. I mean everyone is dropping like flies. Even *you*, Juliette. I mean, imagine that."

"But that beautiful ring?" Juliette's gaze dropped to Kimberly's left hand. She wasn't wearing the ring.

Kimberly made a *pffft* sound. "It was cubic zirconia. Twenty bucks at Target."

Okay, so maybe a leopard couldn't completely change her spots, but it was a huge leap for Kimmy Ogilvie to admit this to Juliette Kingsbury.

It almost felt like an apology.

If not, Juliette was fine. She didn't need anyone's

approval. She finally felt like the leading lady in her own life. That's all that mattered.

"I couldn't believe it at first," Kimberly said, "but eventually, I had to make peace with the fact that Owen has been in love with you for a very long time. I'm so relieved that you two nincompoops finally realized it and got your act together. Take good care of Owen because he really is a good guy. I hope you two will be very happy together."

Juliette didn't know what to say, and it was dawning on her that Kimberly and Dalton Hart had probably worked together to set this up for the scene, because you can only get so far with a parade of subpar wedding gowns.

But it took a lot for the woman to admit all that knowing it would be aired on national television, even if she might have been grabbing the opportunity to be on television. But that wasn't Juliette's concern.

"Thanks, Kimberly," she said. "Owen is a great guy."

A few minutes after Kimberly left the shop, Owen walked in. Helen and Bunny made a fuss over hiding his eyes and bustling Juliette into the fitting room because, as Helen squawked, "It's bad luck for the groom to see his bride in a wedding dress."

"I think the groom is not supposed to see the bride in *the* wedding dress until the ceremony," Juliette said as Helen spread her body over the fitting room curtain, doing her best to ensure that Owen wouldn't see Juliette in white.

"Well, it's best not to take any chances," Bunny called. "There's no sense in that."

As Juliette freed herself of the big gown and dressed in her jeans and blouse, finger combing her curls into place, she smiled to herself.

Another secret—even if it was becoming clear that everyone was in on it—was that Owen's and her love had stood so many tests that it was unlikely a bridal gown that looked like a puff pastry would be their undoing.

When she stepped out of the fitting room, Owen was holding two glasses of champagne that Claudia had given him. He handed one to her.

"I have some news," he said. "Forest said he met with Ed Day, who wants to use Tinsley Cove as a filming location for the next movie he's producing. You should be part of it, Jules. If you want to. I hope you will accept his offer of being the showrunner. Just because we're married doesn't mean you have to give up your dream."

They clinked glasses.

Juliette put her free arm around Owen's neck and kissed him, long and slow.

"I believe my dream is standing right in front of me."

"That's a wrap," Dalton called.

Everyone—Juliette, Owen, Bunny, Helen, Claudia, Dalton and the crew—raised a glass to the bride and groom and dreams come true.

Epilogue

"Places, everyone," Dalton said to Juliette and her four bridesmaids—Tasha, Juliette's future sisters-in-law Cassie and Avery, and Ingrid, who had flown in from Los Angeles. They were gathered in a white tent that had been set up on the beach so that they could stay tucked out of sight of the two hundred and fifty guests who had gathered on Tinsley Cove Beach—the stretch between Helen's house and the home next door, where Owen had lived and first fallen in love with Juliette.

After looking at multiple wedding venues, it seemed only fitting to have the wedding here, in the place where everything had begun. It felt like coming home.

Except for the television crew, but even that was okay.

At first, Juliette and Owen had been adamantly against having their marriage filmed by the *Selling Sandcastle* crew, but after they'd given it some thought, they changed their minds.

They wanted a video recording of their wedding anyway. Why not let an ultra-professional crew do it? Plus, by working with Dalton, rather than trying to subvert him, they were able to set their terms: no ambushes. No making them or anyone in the bridal party look bad. No making a mockery out of their day. It was stated in the contract that they'd signed that if anyone involved in the wedding was portrayed in a negative light, if Dalton manufactured any drama during the days leading up to the wedding and on the day itself, he would be in breach of contract and would not be permitted to use the footage in the show's finale. So far, Dalton had upheld his end of the bargain. Perhaps because this event not only marked the beginning of Owen and Juliette's life together, but it also spelled the end of the *Selling Sandcastle* run, and even Dalton wanted the show to end on a positive note.

It would give Bunny and Bert and the town of Tinsley Cove the closure they all needed as the show they'd all embraced came to an end.

An ending capped off by a beginning.

The beginning of their life together.

The day could not have been more perfect for a beach wedding. Cotton-ball clouds dotted the robin's-egg-blue sky, and the balmy ocean breeze kept everyone cool.

Accompanied by the sound of the wind and the sea and the gulls overhead, the string quartet began playing Pachelbel's "Canon in D Major." Dalton quietly communicated with his crew via microphone and earpiece and cued each of the bridesmaids, one by one, to walk down the aisle.

As Juliette waited for Tasha, her maid of honor, to complete her walk, Juliette said to Dalton, "If television doesn't work out for you, you have a future as a wedding coordinator."

They laughed. "Seriously, thank you for helping make this day special, Dalton."

"Drama might be my second language, but even I know better than to mess with the course of true love." He straightened the crown attached to her veil. "It's your turn, love. Are you ready?"

The butterflies in Juliette's stomach swooped and then flew in formation.

She nodded. She'd been ready for this since the first time she'd set eyes on Owen…even if she hadn't let herself believe it could really happen until they'd pretended to be engaged.

Today, she was marrying the love of her life.

Her soulmate.

Bert had offered to walk Juliette down the aisle. When the quartet began Richard Wagner's "Bridal Chorus" from *Lohengrin* and Dalton gave them the signal, Bert swiped a tear from his eye and offered her his arm.

"Welcome to the family," he said. "Bunny and I couldn't be happier to call you our daughter."

Dalton's assistant straightened out the train of Juliette's elegant A-line silk-and-lace gown, and then Juliette and Bert made their way down the white carpet that had been laid on the sand between two sections of white chairs.

Not a single eye was dry, nor was a single chair empty. They couldn't leave anybody out of their celebration—not even Kimberly, who was there, somewhere in the crowd of well-wishers, with a plus one.

Even though Juliette had intended to take it all in, to memorize every second of this extraordinary day, the walk down the aisle was a blur. The only person she could see was Owen, who was waiting for her at the floral archway that had been erected for their nuptials.

Bert kissed her on the cheek and put her hand in Owen's.

The ceremony was going so fast, but she knew she would never forget the way Owen looked when she reached her position by his side.

"Juliette, I choose you. I choose you to be my partner in life, to have and to hold, in tears and in laughter, in sickness and in health, to love and to cherish, always. From this day forward until the end of time, I will continue to love, honor and respect you."

After Juliette said her vows, Owen slid the diamond band onto her finger.

The officiant said, "By the power vested in me, Owen and Juliette, I now pronounce you husband and wife. You may now share a kiss."

Juliette and Owen smiled at each other, then he pulled her into his arms, kissing her, slow and sweet. For a moment, the rest of the world slipped away...everyone who had gathered on the beach to watch them exchange their vows, the *Selling Sandcastle* crew and their cameras, as unobtrusive and hidden as they tried to be, allowing this day to be about Owen and Juliette, not a television production... Even the roar of the waves, the squawk of the seagulls and the rush of the wind were no match for their moment.

For a glorious moment, they were the only two people in the world.

They had been through so much, but now they were married.

Owen's business was taking off. The SmartScape Technologies smart home system was launching in three months. Juliette had accepted Ed's offer to work on his new picture, which would be filming in Tinsley Cove. After that, time would tell—maybe she would start her own production company.

Time would tell. There was so much waiting for them in the days ahead, and for the first time in a very long time, Juliette was happy where she was—not needing to think several steps ahead. Her future with Owen was real—their love was real—and they had the rest of their lives to be together.

To think it took a fake engagement to bring them to this point. Neither of them had ever been conventional, so why should the lead-up to their happy ending be anything but unconventional?

Except for the music that they'd chosen for the ceremony. They'd gone as traditional as they could for that because it felt right. Just like being in Owen's arms felt right. Planning their life together felt right and real and...wonderful.

As the sounds of *woots* and applause pierced the veil of their moment, they reluctantly pulled apart. They stole one last longing glance at each other before they turned to their friends and family.

"Ladies and gentlemen, I am delighted to present to you, for the very first time, Owen and Juliette Mc-Fadden."

The crowd cheered and whistled, and Juliette held

up her bouquet in a victorious salute as she waited for Tasha to right the train of her gown.

Owen leaned in and whispered, "Are you ready for this, Mrs. McFadden?"

"I've waited my whole life for this, and I can't wait to spend the rest of my life with you, Mr. McFadden."

The beginning notes of Felix Mendelssohn's "Wedding March" started, and Owen stole one more kiss before they took the first step toward the rest of their lives—together.

* * * * *